PANDEMICA
SEP

Become our fan on Facebook **facebook.com/idwpublishing**
Follow us on Twitter **@idwpublishing**
Subscribe to us on YouTube **youtube.com/idwpublishing**
See what's new on Tumblr **tumblr.idwpublishing.com**
Check us out on Instagram **instagram.com/idwpublishing**

IDW
www.IDWPUBLISHING.com

Cover Artist
Esteban Salinas

Series Assistant Editors
Megan Brown
and **Riley Farmer**

Series Editor
David Hedgecock

Collection Editors
Alonzo Simon
and **Zac Boone**

Collection Designer
Claudia Chong

Chris Ryall, President & Publisher/CCO
Cara Morrison, Chief Financial Officer
Matthew Ruzicka, Chief Accounting Officer
David Hedgecock, Associate Publisher
John Barber, Editor-in-Chief
Justin Eisinger, Editorial Director, Graphic Novels and Collections
Jerry Bennington, VP of New Product Development
Lorelei Bunjes, VP of Technology & Information Services
Jud Meyers, Sales Director
Anna Morrow, Marketing Director
Tara McCrillis, Director of Design & Production
Mike Ford, Director of Operations
Shauna Monteforte, Manufacturing Operations Director
Rebekah Cahalin, General Manager

Ted Adams and Robbie Robbins, IDW Founders

ISBN: 978-1-68405-634-7 23 22 21 20 1 2 3 4

Originally published as PANDEMICA issues #1–5.

PANDEMICA

WRITTEN BY
JONATHAN MABERRY

ART BY
ALEX SANCHEZ

COLORS BY
JAY FOTOS

LETTERS BY
SHAWN LEE

ART BY **ALEX SANCHEZ** COLORS BY **JAY FOTOS**

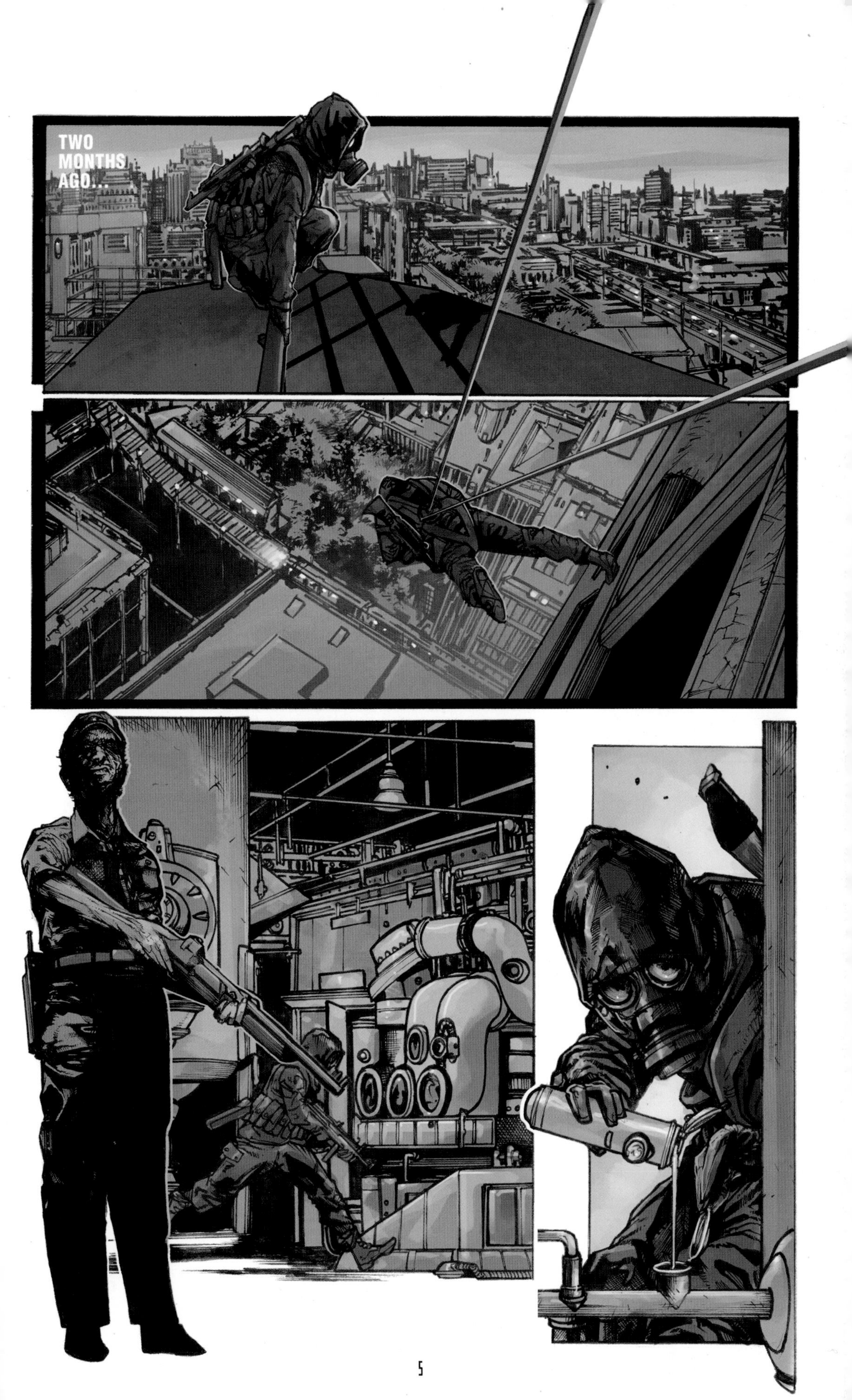
TWO MONTHS AGO...

MISSION ACCOMPLISHED.
PERFECT.
South Texas Detention Complex

NONE OF THE GUARDS HAVE IT. NONE OF THE STAFF... JUST THE DETAINEES...
I... I'VE NEVER SEEN ANYTHING SPREAD THIS FAST.
DEAR GOD...
...CHIKUNGUNYA IS A VIRUS OFTEN SPREAD BY MOSQUITO BITES, WITH THE VICTIMS BEING PRIMARILY PEOPLE IN DEVELOPING NATIONS...
...NORMAL MORTALITY RATE IS LESS THAN ONE IN 1000...
...NEW STRAIN SPREADING LIKE WILDFIRE THROUGH DETENTION CAMPS...
...MORTALITY RATE OF 70%...
...THE ENTIRE MEXICAN BORDER IS BEING CLOSED UNTIL THIS OUTBREAK CAN BE CONTAINED.
BUT GIVEN ITS VIRULENCE, AUTHORITIES ARE SAYING THAT COULD BE WEEKS... OR EVEN MONTHS...
ABSOLUTELY FUCKING PERFECT.

"THE PATTERN OF SPREAD MAKES NO SENSE.
"NOT IF YOU USE ANY MODEL OF CONTAGION WE'VE SEEN. INSTEAD OF INFECTION MOVING OUTWARD FROM A PATIENT ZERO, WE SAW OUTBREAKS IN MULTIPLE PLACES THAT WERE REMOTE FROM EACH OTHER.
"THESE LOCATIONS ARE DEEPLY TROUBLING.
"SUSPICIOUS.
"IMMIGRATION DETENTION FACILITIES ALONG THE BORDER. POORER NEIGHBORHOODS IN MEXICO.
"THROUGHOUT CENTRAL AND SOUTH AMERICA, THE POOREST AREAS OF INDIA. HAITI. PUERTO RICO. GHANA AND NIGERIA.
"AND IN PLACES ACROSS AMERICA. NORTH PHILADELPHIA. WEST BALTIMORE. RACINE. BIRMINGHAM. DETROIT. CHICAGO.
"THE DEATH TOLL AMONG PEOPLE OF COLOR IS WILDLY DISPROPORTIONATE TO WHITE DEATHS."
CDC
OUTBREAKS SPREAD ACROSS RURAL AREA

DR. KATZ, WHEN YOU SAY "DISPROPORTIONATE"... HOW DOES MEDICAL SCIENCE ACCOUNT FOR THIS DISPARITY OF INFECTION?
BREAKS SPREAD ACROSS RURAL AREAS
THAT'S A MYSTERY THAT DEMANDS TO BE SOLVED, EDGAR.
I'VE SEEN A LOT OF EPIDEMICS AND PANDEMICS, AND THE NUMBERS DON'T WORK HERE.
YOU'VE BEEN SAYING THAT A LOT, DR. KATZ. MAKING THE ROUNDS OF EVERY NEWS PROGRAM.
BUT... YOUR COMMENTS GO AGAINST WHAT THE MAJORITY OF EPIDEMIOLOGISTS ARE SAYING.
THAT DEPENDS ON WHO YOU TALK TO, EDGAR.
YOUR COMPETITORS IN THE 24-HOUR NEWS CYCLE HAVE TROTTED OUT A NUMBER OF SO-CALLED EXPERTS TO SAY THAT CHIKUNGUNYA IS A KNOWN DISEASE OF POVERTY.
THAT PREVIOUSLY DOCUMENTED OUTBREAKS IN INDIA, REUNION ISLAND, AND MEXICO CITY ARE PROOF THAT WE'RE SEEING ANOTHER PHASE IN THE LIFE OF THIS DISEASE.
THAT'S NOT WHAT WE'RE SEEING HERE.
I MEAN THAT THERE HAVE BEEN A FEW HUNDRED CAUCASIANS INFECTED IN NORTH AMERICA, AND FROM THAT GROUP A TOTAL OF NINETEEN DEATHS.
WHILE AT THE SAME TIME WE HAVE A DEATH TOLL OF ELEVEN THOUSAND PEOPLE OF COLOR.

THAT'S A BOLD STATEMENT, DR. KATZ.
BOLD? MAYBE. DOESN'T MEAN I'M WRONG.
THERE ARE NATIONS EXPERIENCING OUTBREAKS WHERE THERE IS NO SUBSTANTIAL WHITE DEMOGRAPHIC. DEMOCRATIC REPUBLIC OF CONGO AND GHANA, FOR EXAMPLE.
OKAY, LET'S TALK ABOUT THOSE COUNTRIES.
WHY IS IT THAT THE DISEASE IS ATTACKING ONLY THE YORUBA ETHNIC GROUP, BUT SEEMS TO IGNORE THE FULANI? NONE OF THE TALKING HEAD EXPERTS EVEN TRY TO EXPLAIN THAT.
THE SAME GOES FOR THE CONGOLESE, WHO ARE DYING BY THE THOUSANDS WHILE THE BANTU ARE BARELY TOUCHED. AND WE SEE THE SAME WITH THE ESCALATING MORTALITY AMONG THE TUTSI IN RWANDA, WHILE THE HUTU SEEM TO BE SAFE.
SO... YOU'RE SAYING THAT THE DISEASE FAVORS ONE ETHNICITY OVER ANOTHER, NO MATTER WHERE IT STRIKES.
YES.
HOW IS THAT EVEN POSSIBLE?
IT'S NOT. LOOK, EDGAR, I CANNOT AND WILL NOT BELIEVE THIS IS JUST SOME NATURAL MUTATION.
MOTHER NATURE CAN BE A BITCH, BUT SHE'S NOT A RACIST.
EXCUSE ME, DR. KATZ, BUT ARE YOU ACTUALLY SUGGESTING THAT THIS IS SOME KIND OF DELIBERATE CAMPAIGN OF MASS MURDER?
MASS MURDER? NO. I THINK IT'S FAR WORSE THAN THAT. THIS ISN'T SOME DERANGED PERSON WITH A CHEMISTRY SET.
I BELIEVE WE ARE SEEING SOMETHING FAR WORSE. SOMETHING MUCH MORE DELIBERATE AND NEFARIOUS.
I THINK SOMEONE IS OUT THERE DEVELOPING ETHNIC-SPECIFIC BIOWEAPONS.
I THINK SOMEONE IS OUT THERE SELLING GENOCIDE.

THAT WAS AMAZING, DOC. THE PHONES AND EMAIL ARE EXPLODING. THIS IS GOING TO HIT THE NEWS CYCLE LIKE A CRUISE MISSILE.
GOD, I HOPE SO. WE NEED THE MEDIA TO GET THE WORD OUT.
EVEN VIA THE "FAKE NEWS"?
DON'T EVEN...
...YES, I SAW EVERY GOD DAMN MINUTE OF IT, MOSES. YOU'RE USING YOUR PLATFORM AS ASSISTANT DIRECTOR TO MAKE UNSUBSTANTIATED CLAIMS THAT GO AGAINST DEPARTMENT POLICY.
ARE YOU OUT OF YOUR FUCKING MIND? DO YOU KNOW HOW MANY CONGRESSMEN HAVE ALREADY CALLED ME DEMANDING THAT I FIRE YOU?
YOU DON'T EVEN WANT TO KNOW WHAT THE PRESIDENT IS TWEETING RIGHT NOW.
GLOBAL NETWORK NEWS
TELL YOU WHAT, MURRAY, I CAN SAVE YOU, CONGRESS, AND POTUS A LOT OF GRIEF.
YOU DON'T NEED TO WORRY ABOUT A MEDIA BACKLASH FOR FIRING ME.
AND YOU CAN TAKE A NICE DEEP BREATH AND THEN GO BACK TO SHOVING YOUR NOSE UP THE PRESIDENT'S ASS. I WILL NOT BE PARTY TO A COVER-UP THAT MAKES ME COMPLICIT IN WHOLESALE MURDER.
I HEREBY TENDER MY RESIGNATION.
NOW WAIT A FUCKING MIN—
FUCK OFF.

A LOT OF PEOPLE ARE SAYING YOU WERE FIRED.
I WASN'T.
AND OTHER FOLKS ARE SAYING YOU'RE RUNNING SCARED.
SURE, SO SCARED THAT I'VE BEEN DOING TOWN HALLS AND LIVE INTERVIEWS FOR TWO WEEKS NOW. SO SCARED THAT I'VE HELPED DRAFT DOZENS OF FREEDOM OF INFORMATION FILINGS.
WE NOT ONLY HAVE THE CHIKUNGUNYA... NOW WE'RE SEEING OUTBREAKS OF TAY SACHS AND SICKLE CELL IN NEW AND FRIGHTENING FORMS.
COMMUNICABLE VERSIONS OF THESE THAT ARE TAKING HOLD IN OUR CITIES, IN JEWISH AND BLACK NEIGHBORHOODS.
THIS IS DELIBERATE, AND I WILL GET TO THE BOTTOM OF IT.
HOW? YOU DON'T HAVE THE RESOURCES OF THE CDC. YOU'RE AN OUTSIDER NOW. A PRIVATE CITIZEN.
YOU KNOW WHAT ELSE I AM? RICH. FILTHY RICH. I HAVE MORE MONEY THAN GOD.
I DIDN'T MAKE THAT FORTUNE, I INHERITED IT. AND WHAT IS IT GOOD FOR IF I CAN'T USE IT TO DO SOME GOOD IN THIS WORLD?
SURE, BUT HOW?
I'M FORMING A TEAM OF SPECIALISTS, INVESTIGATORS, DOCTORS, NURSES, CLINICIANS, SCIENTISTS, AND LAWYERS.
WE ARE GOING TO HUNT DOWN THE PEOPLE RESPONSIBLE. THEY ARE MONSTERS. THEY SHOULD BE MADE TO WEAR SIGNS WARNING PEOPLE OF WHAT THEY ARE. WE'LL FIND THEM, OUT THEM, AND HANG THOSE SIGNS AROUND THEIR NECKS. UNCLEAN.

WE NEED THIS TO GO AWAY, LOVERBOY.
GO AWAY BIG OR GO AWAY SMALL?
I DON'T TELL A CHEF HOW TO SEAR A STEAK.
DAD... IF LOVERBOY DOES SOMETHING TO MOSES KATZ, IT'S NOT GOING TO STOP WHAT THAT JEW IS DOING. THE CONSPIRACY THEORISTS AND SOCIAL JUSTICE ACTIVISTS ARE ALREADY RAISING HELL ONLINE.
IF WE KILL THE JEW, THEN THEY'LL KNOW HE WAS RIGHT ALL ALONG. HE'LL BE A MARTYR.
NOT IF IT LOOKS LIKE AN ACCIDENT.
KATZ HAS HAD TWO DWIs IN THE LAST TEN YEARS. HIS WIFE LEFT HIM BECAUSE OF HIS DRINKING. FUCK... I'VE DONE A LOT MORE WITH LESS THAN THAT.
HE WON'T BE A MARTYR, HE'LL BE A DISAPPOINTMENT. THAT'LL CUT THE BALLS OF THAT WHOLE MOVEMENT.
DO IT, LOVERBOY.

LET'S GET THE WHOLE TEAM TOGETHER FOR ORIENTATION FIRST THING TOMORROW.
NO, WE CAN'T WAIT. THERE'S BEEN A NEW STRAIN OF TUBERCULOSIS HITTING THE SYRIAN KURDS. WHATEVER THIS IS, IT'S GETTING WORSE.
OH, ONE GOOD THING. DE'NEESA TEXTED ME. SHE'S AGREED TO MEET. I THINK I CAN GET HER TO SIGN ON.
SHE'S HEADING HERE NOW FROM HER LAST GIG. NO... I HAVE NO IDEA WHERE THAT IS. OR WHAT IT IS. YOU KNOW DE'NEESA. SHE HAS THAT JSOC* WAY OF TELLING YOU EXACTLY JACK SHIT.
*JOINT SPECIAL OPERATIONS COMMAND.
BUT I'LL FEEL A LOT SAFER WITH HER WATCHING MY–SHIT!
HEY! WATCH WHERE THE FUCK YOU'RE–
OH MY GOD... OH MY GOD... OH MY GOD...

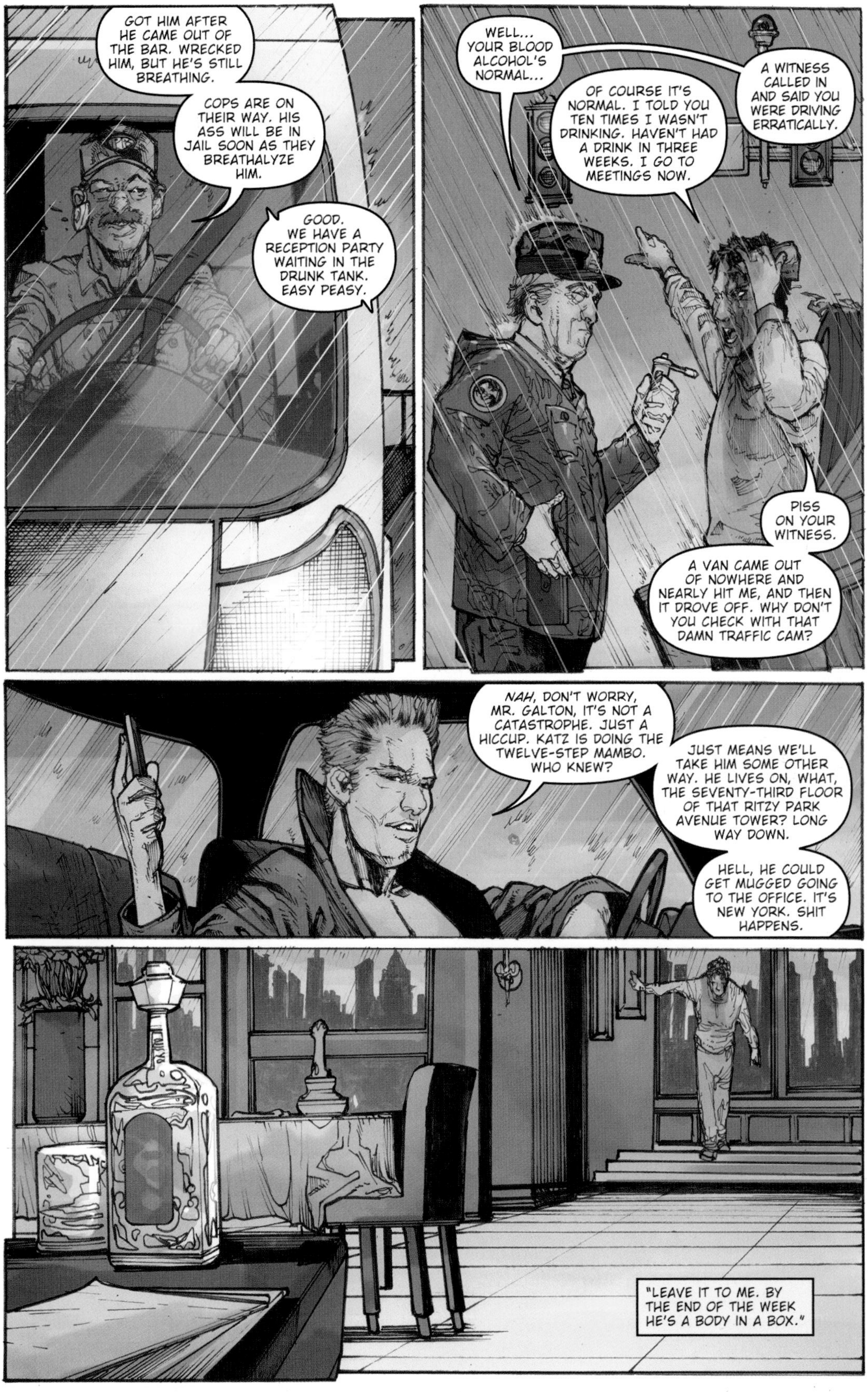
GOT HIM AFTER HE CAME OUT OF THE BAR. WRECKED HIM, BUT HE'S STILL BREATHING.
COPS ARE ON THEIR WAY. HIS ASS WILL BE IN JAIL SOON AS THEY BREATHALYZE HIM.
GOOD. WE HAVE A RECEPTION PARTY WAITING IN THE DRUNK TANK. EASY PEASY.
WELL... YOUR BLOOD ALCOHOL'S NORMAL...
A WITNESS CALLED IN AND SAID YOU WERE DRIVING ERRATICALLY.
OF COURSE IT'S NORMAL. I TOLD YOU TEN TIMES I WASN'T DRINKING. HAVEN'T HAD A DRINK IN THREE WEEKS. I GO TO MEETINGS NOW.
PISS ON YOUR WITNESS.
A VAN CAME OUT OF NOWHERE AND NEARLY HIT ME, AND THEN IT DROVE OFF. WHY DON'T YOU CHECK WITH THAT DAMN TRAFFIC CAM?
NAH, DON'T WORRY, MR. GALTON, IT'S NOT A CATASTROPHE. JUST A HICCUP. KATZ IS DOING THE TWELVE-STEP MAMBO. WHO KNEW?
JUST MEANS WE'LL TAKE HIM SOME OTHER WAY. HE LIVES ON, WHAT, THE SEVENTY-THIRD FLOOR OF THAT RITZY PARK AVENUE TOWER? LONG WAY DOWN.
HELL, HE COULD GET MUGGED GOING TO THE OFFICE. IT'S NEW YORK. SHIT HAPPENS.
"LEAVE IT TO ME. BY THE END OF THE WEEK HE'S A BODY IN A BOX."

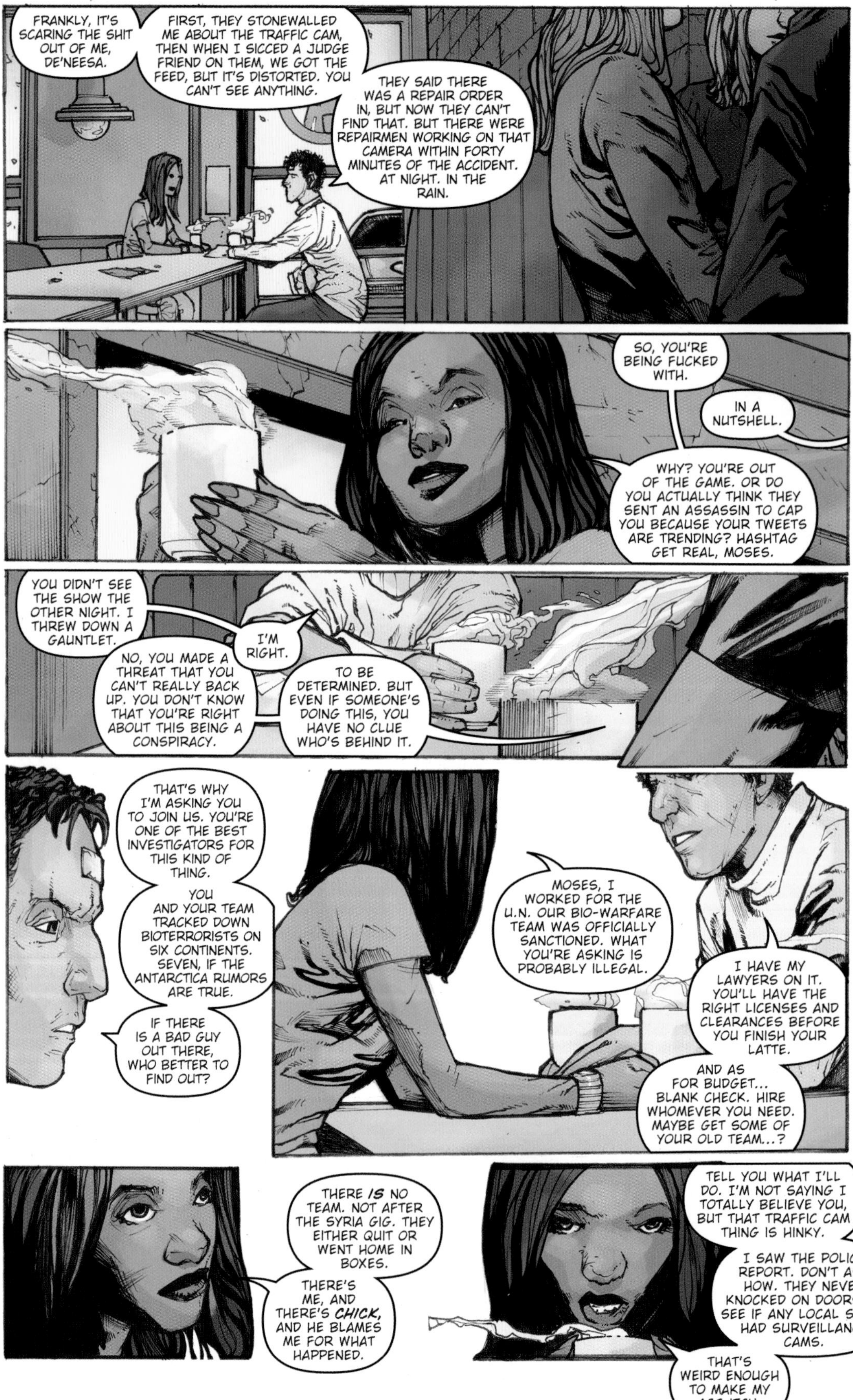
FRANKLY, IT'S SCARING THE SHIT OUT OF ME, DE'NEESA.
FIRST, THEY STONEWALLED ME ABOUT THE TRAFFIC CAM, THEN WHEN I SICCED A JUDGE FRIEND ON THEM, WE GOT THE FEED, BUT IT'S DISTORTED. YOU CAN'T SEE ANYTHING.
THEY SAID THERE WAS A REPAIR ORDER IN, BUT NOW THEY CAN'T FIND THAT. BUT THERE WERE REPAIRMEN WORKING ON THAT CAMERA WITHIN FORTY MINUTES OF THE ACCIDENT. AT NIGHT. IN THE RAIN.
SO, YOU'RE BEING FUCKED WITH.
IN A NUTSHELL.
WHY? YOU'RE OUT OF THE GAME. OR DO YOU ACTUALLY THINK THEY SENT AN ASSASSIN TO CAP YOU BECAUSE YOUR TWEETS ARE TRENDING? HASHTAG GET REAL, MOSES.
YOU DIDN'T SEE THE SHOW THE OTHER NIGHT. I THREW DOWN A GAUNTLET.
I'M RIGHT.
NO, YOU MADE A THREAT THAT YOU CAN'T REALLY BACK UP. YOU DON'T KNOW THAT YOU'RE RIGHT ABOUT THIS BEING A CONSPIRACY.
TO BE DETERMINED. BUT EVEN IF SOMEONE'S DOING THIS, YOU HAVE NO CLUE WHO'S BEHIND IT.
THAT'S WHY I'M ASKING YOU TO JOIN US. YOU'RE ONE OF THE BEST INVESTIGATORS FOR THIS KIND OF THING.
YOU AND YOUR TEAM TRACKED DOWN BIOTERRORISTS ON SIX CONTINENTS. SEVEN, IF THE ANTARCTICA RUMORS ARE TRUE.
IF THERE IS A BAD GUY OUT THERE, WHO BETTER TO FIND OUT?
MOSES, I WORKED FOR THE U.N. OUR BIO-WARFARE TEAM WAS OFFICIALLY SANCTIONED. WHAT YOU'RE ASKING IS PROBABLY ILLEGAL.
I HAVE MY LAWYERS ON IT. YOU'LL HAVE THE RIGHT LICENSES AND CLEARANCES BEFORE YOU FINISH YOUR LATTE.
AND AS FOR BUDGET... BLANK CHECK. HIRE WHOMEVER YOU NEED. MAYBE GET SOME OF YOUR OLD TEAM...?
THERE *IS* NO TEAM. NOT AFTER THE SYRIA GIG. THEY EITHER QUIT OR WENT HOME IN BOXES.
THERE'S ME, AND THERE'S ***CHICK,*** AND HE BLAMES ME FOR WHAT HAPPENED.
TELL YOU WHAT I'LL DO. I'M NOT SAYING I TOTALLY BELIEVE YOU, BUT THAT TRAFFIC CAM THING IS HINKY.
I SAW THE POLICE REPORT. DON'T ASK HOW. THEY NEVER KNOCKED ON DOORS T SEE IF ANY LOCAL STO HAD SURVEILLANCE CAMS.
THAT'S WEIRD ENOUGH TO MAKE MY ASS ITCH.

IF THERE'S ANYTHING TO BE FOUND, THEN I'LL FIND IT.
YES, MISS. I HEARD THE ACCIDENT, BUT SINCE THE POLICE WERE THERE RIGHT AWAY, I NEVER THOUGHT TO TELL THEM ABOUT MY CAMERA.
NO PROBLEM, MR. SINGH.
COULD I TAKE A LOOK AT THE VIDEO LOG FROM THAT NIGHT?
OF COURSE, OF COURSE.
MOSES? NOT SAYING YOU'RE NOT CRAZY, BUT AT LEAST YOU'RE NOT WRONG.
GOT ENOUGH TO START AN INVESTIGATION. WHITE VAN, LIKE YOU SAID. INARGUABLE. AND A GOOD TECH MIGHT BE ABLE TO PULL THE FACE OF THE DRIVER. I KNOW A GUY.
OOOOMPH!
SORRY, BITCH.
WHAT DID YOU SAY?

CRACK
MARTY'S GARAGE
AT YOUR SERVICE
POP-
POP

BLAM
NO...
LOVERBOY?
SKREEEEE

AND I'M TELLING YOU, HE'S NOT DEAD.
LISTEN, CHICK... THAT WAS HIM IN THE VAN. NO DOUBT ABOUT IT. THAT SAME SHIT-EATING SMILE.
WE BOTH SAW HIM DIE, DE'NEESA. THAT WHOLE BUILDING CAME DOWN ON HIS HEAD. FUCK, HE DIED TO MAKE SURE WE GOT OUT.
UNLESS HE'S A FUCKING ZOMBIE, THAT CAN'T HAVE BEEN HIM YOU SAW.
REMEMBER THE WAY WE TOOK THAT BRIEFCASE AWAY FROM THE RUSSIAN PHARMACOLOGIST? THAT WAS ONE OF LOVERBOY'S TRICKS.
THIS WAS EXACTLY THE SAME PLAY. THREE STREET PEOPLE HITTING IN A THREE-POINT CLOSE, WITH A SHOOTER LAYING DOWN SUPPRESSING FIRE.
SHIT.
SHIT, SHIT, SHIT.
I KNOW.
LOVERBOY'S DEATH BROKE THE TEAM APART. BROKE US APART. NOW WE KNOW IT WAS HIM RUNNING SOME KIND OF GAME.
WHICH MAKES US A COUPLE OF PATSIES.
SHIT, D, I BLAMED YOU FOR WHAT HAPPENED. I HATED YOU FOR IT.
AND ALL THIS TIME THE MOTHERFUCKER WAS ALIVE.
HE WAS LIKE MY BROTHER. I MOURNED FOR HIM. I LOST YOU BECAUSE OF HIM.
NOW I WANT TO BEAT THE FUCK OUT OF HIM UNTIL HE TELLS US WHY.
AND THEN I WANT TO KILL HIM.

BESIDES, D, I THINK WE MIGHT BE PULLING ON TWO ENDS OF THE SAME STRING.
WHAT DO YOU MEAN, CHICK?
YOU SAY THIS MOSES KATZ GUY THINKS THERE'S SOME KIND OF CONSPIRACY?
SURE... WHY?
BECAUSE MY TEAM JUST BUSTED SOME BANTU COCKSUCKERS WHO WERE TRYING TO DUMP SOME REAL INTERESTING SHIT INTO A WELL IN A CONGOLESE VILLAGE.
GOT BIOHAZARD STICKERS ALL OVER IT.
I'LL BE ON THE FIRST PLANE OUT OF HERE TONIGHT. BUT FIRST I WANT TO HAVE A MEANINGFUL CHAT WITH THE LAST FEW ASSHOLES WE DIDN'T SHOOT.
BET THESE FUCKERS WANT TO GET RIGHT WITH JESUS, OR MOHAMMAD, OR WHOEVER THEY PRAY TO, BECAUSE THIS IS GOING TO BE A RELIGIOUS MOMENT FOR THEM.
I CAN DANG-SURE GUARANTEE IT.
BOY HOWDY, YES I CAN.

THANK YOU ALL FOR COMING HERE.
BUT AS OF THIS MORNING, THE DEATH TOLL IN THE UNITED STATES HAS HIT TWELVE THOUSAND.
GLOBALLY, COUNTING DEATHS FROM THE FOURTEEN DIFFERENT UNEXPLAINED EPIDEMICS, WE ESTIMATE THAT OVER NINETY THOUSAND HAVE DIED.
WE HAVE TO STOP THIS. NO ONE ELSE THINKS THIS IS A WAR. I DO. WE DO.
I KNOW I'M ASKING A LOT OF EACH OF YOU. TIME. EFFORT. AND SOME RISK. MAYBE A LOT OF RISK.
DE'NEESA HERE WILL BE OUR CHIEF OF SECURITY.
SHE AND HER FORMER PARTNER, CHARLIE WEED, KNOWN AS CHICK, WERE PART OF A U.N. SPECIAL OPS TEAM SPECIALIZING IN THE HUNT FOR PERSONS, GROUPS, OR GOVERNMENTS USING DESIGNER BIOWEAPONS.
THEY ARE UNIQUELY QUALIFIED TO BE THE TIP OF THE SPEAR FOR US.

"CHICK IS ON HIS WAY HERE FROM AFRICA AND HE HAS PROOF–ACTUAL PROOF–THAT THIS IS NOT A NATURAL DISASTER. THAT THIS IS DELIBERATE. THAT THIS IS MURDER.
"WE DON'T KNOW WHY. WE DON'T KNOW WHO IS BEHIND IT.
"BUT WE WILL FIND OUT.
"AND–TOGETHER–WE WILL TEAR THEM DOWN."
JESUS CHRIST, LOVERBOY... INSTEAD OF STOPPING THAT LITTLE JEW AND HIS FRIENDS, NOW THEY'RE A GODDAMN ARMY.
IF THIS CHICK PERSON HAS PROOF–SAMPLES FROM WHAT WE SOLD TO THE BANTU–THEY COULD REVERSE ENGINEER IT. THEY MIGHT FIGURE IT OUT.
DON'T GET YOUR PANTIES IN A KNOT, JENN. IT DOESN'T MATTER. NONE OF IT DOES.
BY THE TIME THEY FIGURE OUT WHAT'S HAPPENING, THEY'LL BE DROWNING IN THEIR OWN BLOOD.

SOON.
"EVERYTHING'S GOING TO WORK OUT JUST FINE."

ART BY **ALEX SANCHEZ** COLORS BY **JAY FOTOS**

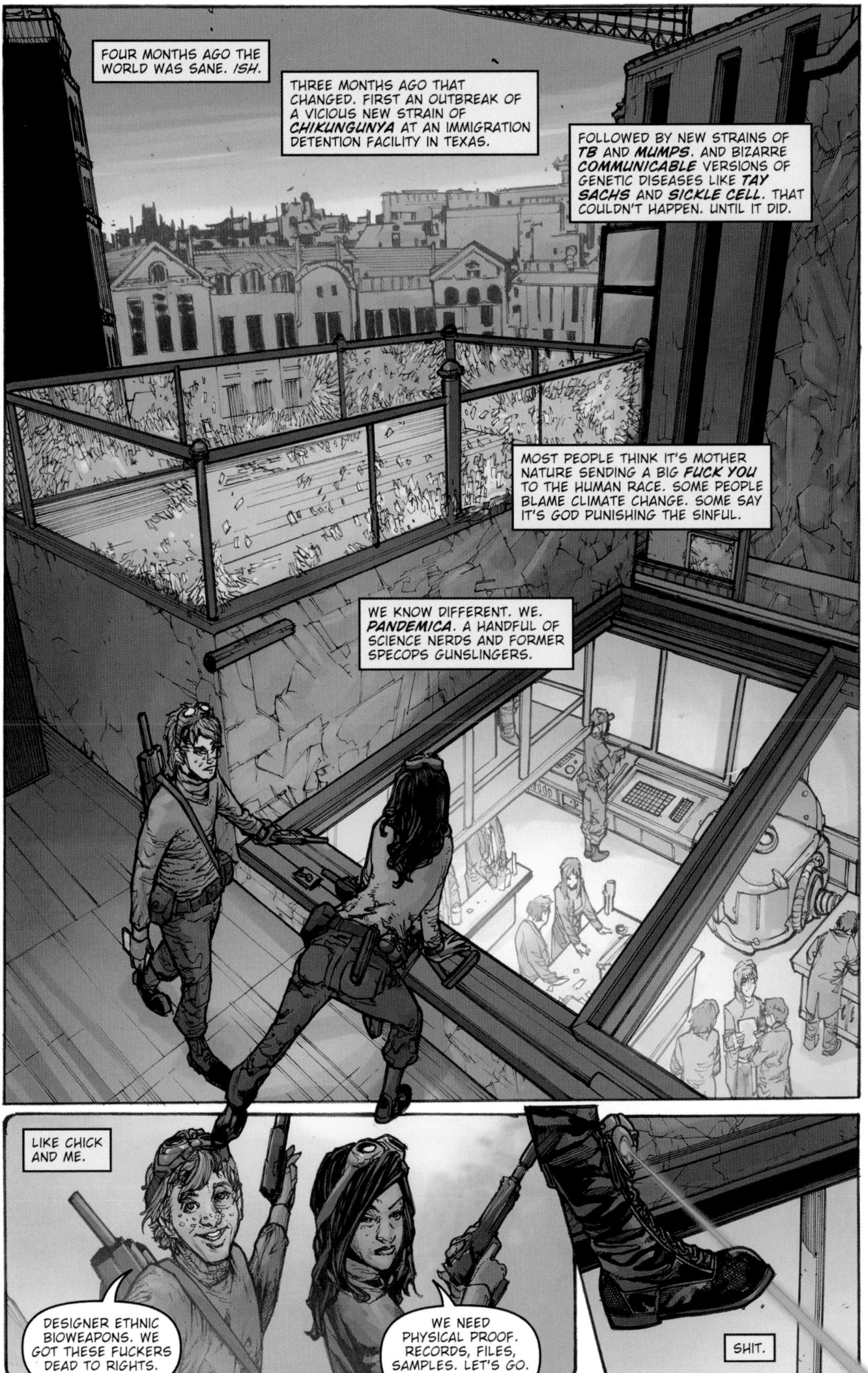

FOUR MONTHS AGO THE WORLD WAS SANE. *ISH.*
THREE MONTHS AGO THAT CHANGED. FIRST AN OUTBREAK OF A VICIOUS NEW STRAIN OF ***CHIKUNGUNYA*** AT AN IMMIGRATION DETENTION FACILITY IN TEXAS.
FOLLOWED BY NEW STRAINS OF ***TB*** AND ***MUMPS***. AND BIZARRE ***COMMUNICABLE*** VERSIONS OF GENETIC DISEASES LIKE ***TAY SACHS*** AND ***SICKLE CELL***. THAT COULDN'T HAPPEN. UNTIL IT DID.
MOST PEOPLE THINK IT'S MOTHER NATURE SENDING A BIG ***FUCK YOU*** TO THE HUMAN RACE. SOME PEOPLE BLAME CLIMATE CHANGE. SOME SAY IT'S GOD PUNISHING THE SINFUL.
WE KNOW DIFFERENT. WE. ***PANDEMICA***. A HANDFUL OF SCIENCE NERDS AND FORMER SPECOPS GUNSLINGERS.
LIKE CHICK AND ME.
DESIGNER ETHNIC BIOWEAPONS. WE GOT THESE FUCKERS DEAD TO RIGHTS.
WE NEED PHYSICAL PROOF. RECORDS, FILES, SAMPLES. LET'S GO.
SHIT.

KRA-BANG
WE DON'T KNOW WHO THESE PEOPLE ARE. OR WHY THEY'RE DOING THIS. THEY'RE RESPONSIBLE FOR NEARLY 800,000 DEATHS WORLDWIDE.
POKA-POKA-POKA-
WE'RE NOT HERE TO ASK NICELY.
HEY, GENIUS! STOP FUCKING SHOOTING GUNS IN A BIOWEAPONS LAB!
CRACK
IT'S NOT THAT YOU CAN'T, CHICK. IT'S ALL A MATTER OF WHAT YOU'RE LOADED WITH AND HOW YOU PICK YOUR TARGETS.
THWOP
.22 CALIBER, LIGHT LOADS. THERE'S A REASON IT'S THE WEAPON OF CHOICE BY YOUR FINEST INTERNATIONAL ASSASSINS. NO EXIT WOUNDS.

THE GUARDS ARE RENTED MUSCLE. THEY WON'T HAVE THE RIGHT ANSWERS.
TRULY SUCKS TO BE THEM.
CHICK! WE NEED THE SCIENTISTS ALIVE.
KIND OF NEED TO BE ALIVE MY OWNSELF.
THEN KILL EVERYONE WITH A GUN.
WORKS FOR ME. *YIPPIE-KI-YAY!*

MULTIPLE YIELD A
NO! DON'T KILL ME! PLEASE I WAS JUST—
—IF THE REST OF THAT SENTENCE IS "FOLLOWING ORDERS", I'LL CUT YOUR BALLS OFF.
SHE WILL, TOO. I SPEAK FROM EXPERIENCE WHEN I SAY YOU DO NOT WANT TO PISS HER OFF.
NO ONE STILL ALIVE EVER HAS. FEEL ME?
...THEY CALL THEMSELVES THE ARK. DON'T KNOW IF THAT'S AN ACRONYM. MIGHT BE BIBLICAL.
THEY HAVE... UM... THINGS TO HOLD OVER US. EVIDENCE OF PAST INDISCRETIONS. PHOTOS. YOU KNOW. THEY OWN US. BODY AND SOUL.
THEY'VE FORCED US TO WORK ON THESE NEW DISEASE FORMS. RADICAL STUFF. MUTANT STRAINS. EDITED GENES.
GET TO THE FUCKING POINT. WHAT ARE YOU MAKING AND WHY?
THEY GAVE US BULK DATA AND SAMPLES FROM ALL OVER. LIKE HARVESTER—A BACTERIAL PLAGUE DESIGNED BY JOSEF MENGELE AS A WAY OF SELECTIVELY TARGETING ASHKENAZI JEWS. WE REFINED IT AND MADE IT PRACTICAL.
ALGHUL, WHICH WE ENGINEERED TO TARGET CERTAIN ARAB POPULATIONS...
...GRAY DRAGON... DEVELOPED BY THE RUSSIANS DURING THEIR CONFLICTS WITH CHINA... PERFECTED BY US FOR ARK...
...TOTEM... CREATED FOR EXECUTIVES IN OIL COMPANIES TO ACQUIRE LANDS POPULATED BY NATIVE AMERICANS. AND...

HE TALKED AND TALKED AND TALKED. SPEAKING HORRORS. AND DESPITE HIS FEAR, THERE WAS A SENSE OF PRIDE. GOD HELP US.

IT'S NOT ME, YOU UNDERSTAND. THEY HAVE THOSE PHOTOS. THEY *OWN* ME.
TAKE THE RECORDS, THE FILES. EVERYTHING.
SPLUT
SHIT!
NO!
THE ALLEY... *GO!*
THWOP
THWOP THWOP
WELL FUCK ME BLIND AND MOVE THE FURNITURE...

WELL... AT LEAST WE HAVE THE ENTIRE LAB.
COMPUTERS, SAMPLES, THE WORKS.
WE'LL BREAK THIS THING WIDE OPEN.
BA-DA-DOOM

WITHOUT RECORDS FROM THAT LAB WE HAVE ONLY WHAT THE ARK SCIENTIST TOLD DE AND CHICK. WHERE DOES THAT LEAVE US, DR. COLE?
IN TROUBLE AND A BIT CONFUSED.
THE FACT THAT WE'VE ALREADY SEEN GENETIC DISORDERS LIKE TAY SACHS AND SICKLE CELL ENGINEERED INTO FAST-ONSET COMMUNICABLE DISEASES PUSHES BACK THE LIMITS OF KNOWN SCIENCE.
A LOT OF THINGS IN SCIENCE ARE THEORETICALLY POSSIBLE.
THE BARRIER IS GENERALLY FUNDING.
WE HAVE PROOF SOMEONE IS SINKING MILLIONS INTO R&D.
THEY'RE BYPASSING NORMAL VECTORS SUCH AS MOSQUITOES—AS WITH CHIKUNGUNYA—OR GENERATIONAL GENETICS TO CREATE TRUE BIOWEAPONS.
I SUSPECT THEY'RE USING ***VIRUSES*** AS ***DELIVERY SYSTEMS*** AND ***CRISPR GENE-EDITING*** TO TARGET ***ETHNIC DNA MARKERS***.
PANDEMICA IS UNOFFICIAL. WE CAN'T PUT IN REQUESTS FOR SAMPLES.
CHICK AND I MIGHT BE ABLE TO FINAGLE SOMETHING. AND BEFORE YOU ASK HOW... DON'T.
THAT'S NOT ALL WE NEED TO WORRY ABOUT.
LOVERBOY'S ONE OF THE MOST DANGEROUS PEOPLE I'VE EVER MET. IF HE'S WORKING FOR THIS ARK THING, THEN WE'RE SERIOUSLY FUCKED. IN THE ASS. WITHOUT LUBE.

I'LL SEE YOUR PSYCHO KILLER AND RAISE YOU RANDOM AND UNPREDICTABLE MUTATIONS.
BECAUSE THESE ARE BIOWEAPONS AND NOT ACTUAL MEDICINES OR APPROVED TREATMENTS, YOU CAN BET THAT THESE ARK PEOPLE HAVEN'T DONE EXTENSIVE HUMAN TRIALS TO IDENTIFY POSSIBLE ADVERSE EXPERIENCES.
I'VE BEEN COLLECTING SOME REPORTS OF PEOPLE PRESENTING AT ERS WITH ANOMALOUS SYMPTOMS. AND NOT JUST THE PEOPLE IN ARK'S APPARENT TARGET DEMOGRAPHICS.
IT'S ONLY A MATTER OF TIME BEFORE WE BEGIN SEEING **EXTREME MUTATIONS**.
"WHO KNOWS WHAT'S GOING TO HAPPEN WHEN THESE DISEASES COLLIDE. ESPECIALLY IN AREAS WITH MIXED-RACE POPULATIONS.
"YOU THINK WE'VE SEEN HORRORS?
"GOD HELP US, BUT I'M AFRAID WE HAVEN'T SEEN HOW **BAD** THIS COULD GET."
OXFORD
ROOSEVELT

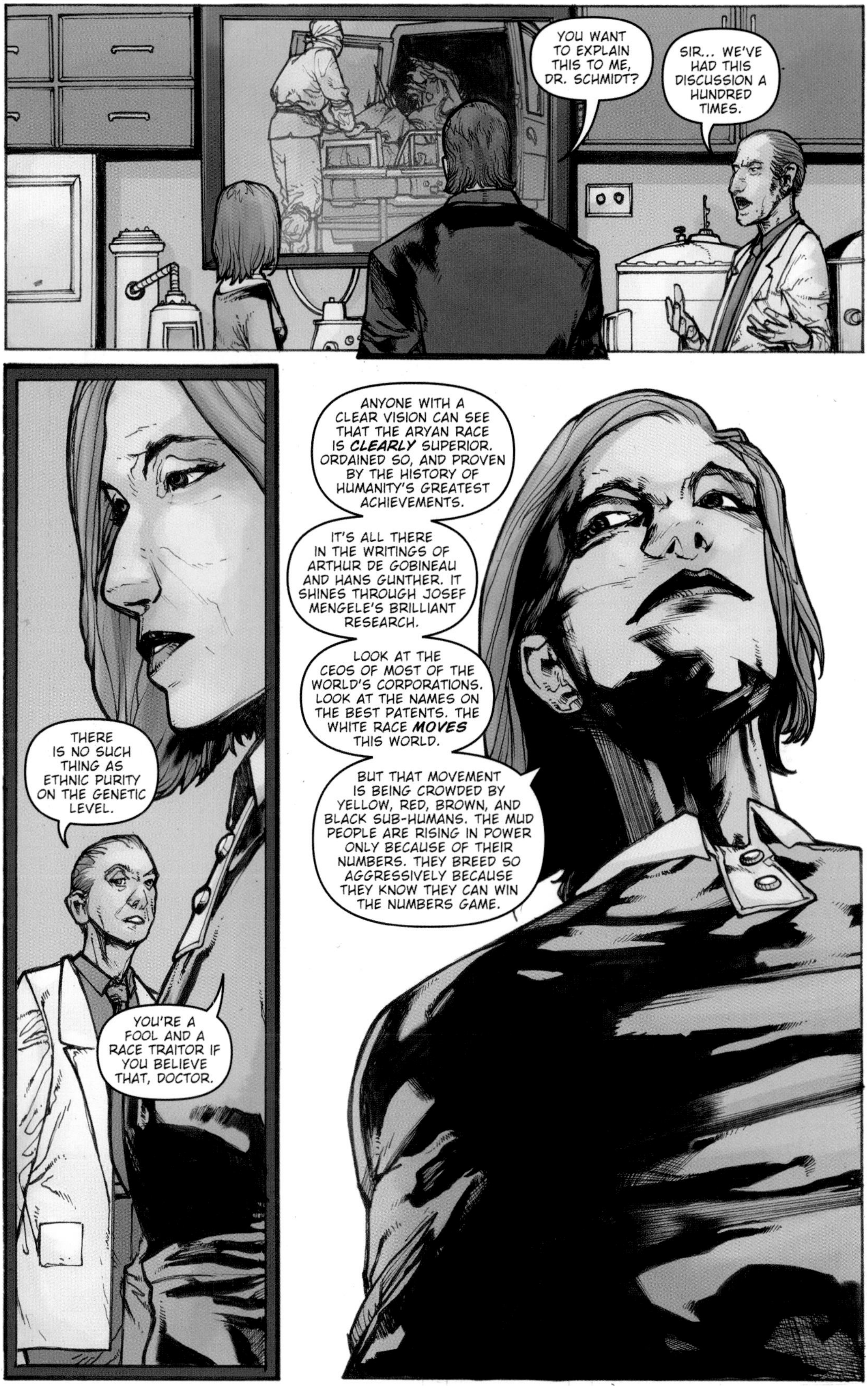

YOU WANT TO EXPLAIN THIS TO ME, DR. SCHMIDT?
SIR... WE'VE HAD THIS DISCUSSION A HUNDRED TIMES.
THERE IS NO SUCH THING AS ETHNIC PURITY ON THE GENETIC LEVEL.
YOU'RE A FOOL AND A RACE TRAITOR IF YOU BELIEVE THAT, DOCTOR.
ANYONE WITH A CLEAR VISION CAN SEE THAT THE ARYAN RACE IS *CLEARLY* SUPERIOR. ORDAINED SO, AND PROVEN BY THE HISTORY OF HUMANITY'S GREATEST ACHIEVEMENTS.
IT'S ALL THERE IN THE WRITINGS OF ARTHUR DE GOBINEAU AND HANS GUNTHER. IT SHINES THROUGH JOSEF MENGELE'S BRILLIANT RESEARCH.
LOOK AT THE CEOS OF MOST OF THE WORLD'S CORPORATIONS. LOOK AT THE NAMES ON THE BEST PATENTS. THE WHITE RACE *MOVES* THIS WORLD.
BUT THAT MOVEMENT IS BEING CROWDED BY YELLOW, RED, BROWN, AND BLACK SUB-HUMANS. THE MUD PEOPLE ARE RISING IN POWER ONLY BECAUSE OF THEIR NUMBERS. THEY BREED SO AGGRESSIVELY BECAUSE THEY KNOW THEY CAN WIN THE NUMBERS GAME.

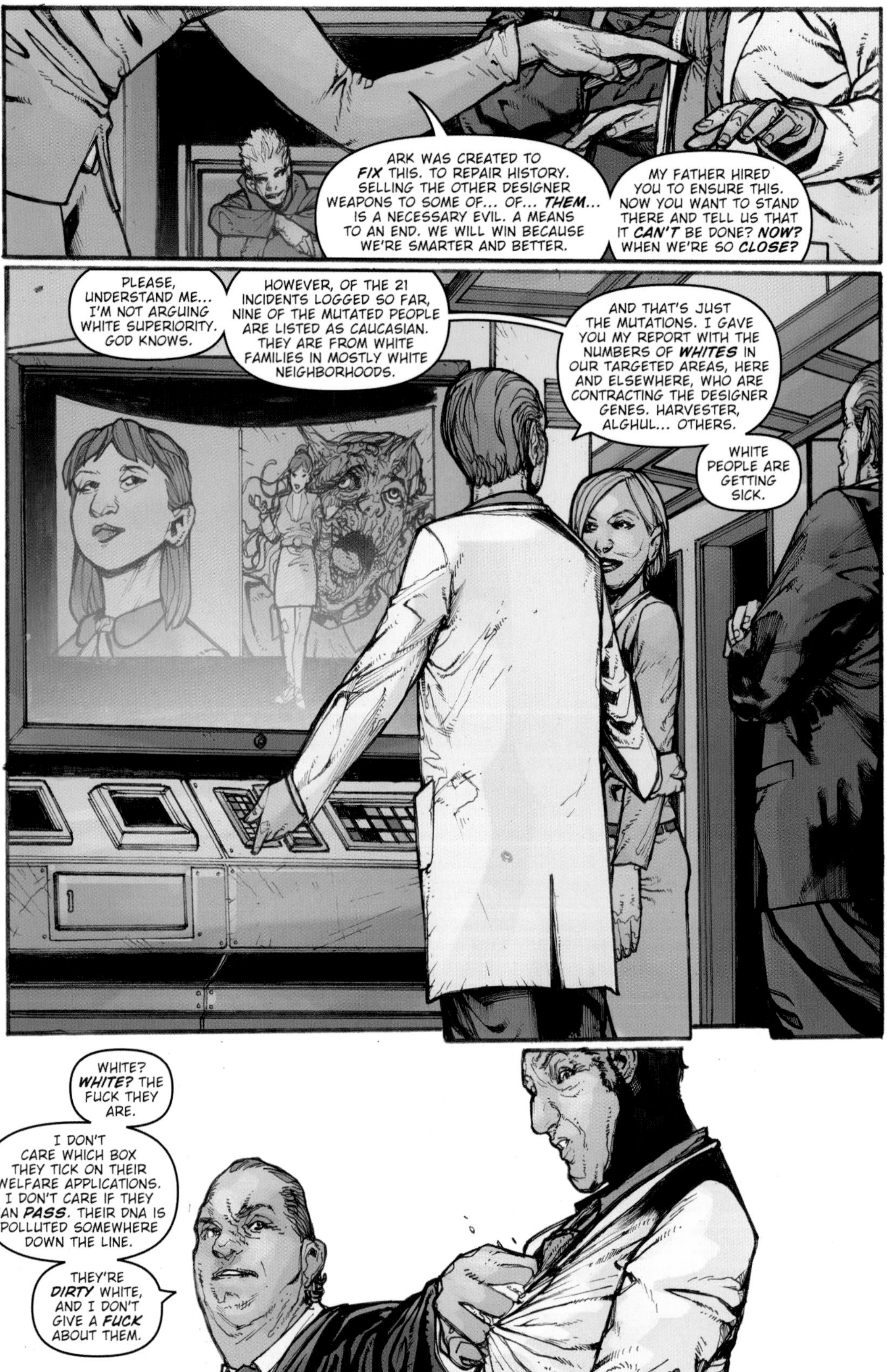
ARK WAS CREATED TO FIX THIS. TO REPAIR HISTORY. SELLING THE OTHER DESIGNER WEAPONS TO SOME OF... OF... THEM... IS A NECESSARY EVIL. A MEANS TO AN END. WE WILL WIN BECAUSE WE'RE SMARTER AND BETTER.
MY FATHER HIRED YOU TO ENSURE THIS. NOW YOU WANT TO STAND THERE AND TELL US THAT IT CAN'T BE DONE? NOW? WHEN WE'RE SO CLOSE?
PLEASE, UNDERSTAND ME... I'M NOT ARGUING WHITE SUPERIORITY. GOD KNOWS.
HOWEVER, OF THE 21 INCIDENTS LOGGED SO FAR, NINE OF THE MUTATED PEOPLE ARE LISTED AS CAUCASIAN. THEY ARE FROM WHITE FAMILIES IN MOSTLY WHITE NEIGHBORHOODS.
AND THAT'S JUST THE MUTATIONS. I GAVE YOU MY REPORT WITH THE NUMBERS OF WHITES IN OUR TARGETED AREAS, HERE AND ELSEWHERE, WHO ARE CONTRACTING THE DESIGNER GENES. HARVESTER, ALGHUL... OTHERS.
WHITE PEOPLE ARE GETTING SICK.
WHITE? WHITE? THE FUCK THEY ARE.
I DON'T CARE WHICH BOX THEY TICK ON THEIR WELFARE APPLICATIONS. I DON'T CARE IF THEY CAN PASS. THEIR DNA IS POLLUTED SOMEWHERE DOWN THE LINE.
THEY'RE DIRTY WHITE, AND I DON'T GIVE A FUCK ABOUT THEM.

I'M NOT REALLY A FIELD GUY, MOSES.
OH, UNCLENCH, RON. THE FIELD IS WHERE IT'S AT. THE FIELD IS WHERE WE STEP OUT OF THEORY AND INTO LIVING SCIENCE.
IT'S WHERE WE GET TO MAKE A DIFFERENCE...
...STILL TIME...

FALL BACK! FALL BACK!

BIOHAZARD CAUTION BIOHAZARD
CAUTION
ON BIOHAZARD CAUTION

WHAT TRULY STAGGERS ME IS THE LEVEL OF AGGRESSIVE STUPIDITY RAMPANT IN OUR GOVERNMENT. BOTH SIDES OF THE DAMN AISLE.
WE HAVE NINETY-THREE DEAD IN PHILLY. ALMOST AS MANY IN THE SUBURBS. WE HAVE OUTBREAKS OF RADICAL DISEASE FORMS IN THIRTY-TWO STATES.
AND THEY'RE CALLING IT A NATURAL DISASTER.
HOW IS ANY OF THIS ***NATURAL?*** EVEN TO THE MEANEST INTELLIGENCE?
MUCH AS I'D LIKE TO BELIEVE THIS IS JUST NAIVETY ON THE PART OF CONGRESS, I'M TOO MUCH OF A CYNIC TO BUY IT.
ARK BLACKMAILED THE SCIENTISTS AT THAT LAB. MAYBE THEY HAVE STUFF ON KEY PEOPLE IN WASHINGTON.
SURE. EVERY OTHER DAY ONE OF THEM'S GETTING CAUGHT WITH THEIR DICK STUCK IN THE WRONG HOLE. GOT TO BE PHOTOS OF SOME OF THAT SHIT.
AND LET'S NOT FORGET THE RICH HISTORY OF BRIBERY IN GLOBAL POLITICS.
DOC, SURELY THERE'S SOMETHING WE CAN USE TO PROVE THAT THESE ARE ACTUALLY BIOWEAPONS.
HARD EVIDENCE WE CAN SHOW TO THE PRESS, BLAST ON SOCIAL MEDIA, TAKE TO THE U.N.

MAYBE...
...I'VE BEEN PUZZLING OVER THE FACT THAT A DISPROPORTIONATELY LOW NUMBER OF GUARDS AND OFFICIALS IN SOME LOCATIONS HAVE GOTTEN SICK.
THE NUMBERS DON'T WORK FOR THAT TO BE RANDOM, WHICH IS SUGGESTIVE OF SOME KIND OF PROPHYLAXIS.
LIKE WHAT? MOST OF THOSE STAFF MEMBERS ARE WHITE.
ISN'T THAT ENOUGH OF A SAFEGUARD AGAINST ETHNIC-SPECIFIC PATHOGENS?
NO, I CAN SEE WHERE THE DOC'S GOING WITH THIS.
BEING WHITE ISN'T ENOUGH. NOT EVEN WITH GENETICALLY ALTERED DISEASES.
EXACTLY. WE'RE SEEING EVIDENCE OF INFLUENZA IN MOST OF THE VICTIMS, EVEN IF IT ISN'T FLU THAT'S MAKING THEM SICK. I BELIEVE THAT'S JUST THE DELIVERY SYSTEM.
SO MAYBE WE SHOULD LOOK AT THE BLOOD OF THE PEOPLE WHO ARE *NOT* GETTING SICK TO SEE IF THEY'VE VACCINATED AGAINST THE WEAPONIZED VIRUS.
IF THEY'VE BEEN VACCINATED, RON, THEY'RE NOT JUST GOING TO LET US DRAW BLOOD. AND THE COURTS WOULD BACK THEM ON REFUSAL.
WHY DON'T YOU LEAVE THAT TO US.
IF YOU WANT BLOOD SAMPLES...
...WE CAN GET THEM TO BLEED FOR US.

GOD! THAT'S BILL VANDERBERG. YOU WENT TO SCHOOL WITH HIM, DAD.
AS I SAID, MR. GALTON, IT'S SPREADING.
VERY WELL.
WE STILL HAVE BLOODHOUND LOCKED AND LOADED, YES?
YES, BUT, PLEASE, MR. GALTON, I HAVE TO CAUTION YOU AGAINST EVEN CONSIDERING RELEASING BLOODHOUND.
HE... HE'S RIGHT, DAD. SURE, IT MIGHT STOP THE MUTATIONS, BUT IT MIGHT ALSO SPREAD TO THE ALL-WHITE POPULATION, TOO.
THAT'S THE POINT. WE DON'T KNOW.
I KNOW.
I KNOW FOR DAMN SURE.
GOD MADE THE WHITE MAN IN HIS OWN IMAGE.
AND GOD WILL PROTECT HIS CHILDREN.
BLOODHOUND. I LOVE THAT NAME. WELL, I'VE WANTED TO SAY THIS MY WHOLE DAMN LIFE—
RELEASE THE HOUNDS.

SOON...
THE WORLD ISN'T THE WORLD ANYMORE.
THE DEVIL'S OFF THE LEASH. HOPE'S BLEEDING ON THE FLOOR.
AND WE ARE WELL AND TRULY FUCKED.
HOPE IS DOWN, BUT IT'S NOT DEAD.

CLICK
FUCK.
HEY, BROWN SUGAR. BEEN LOOKING FOR YOU FOR A LONG DAMN TIME.
HELL, EVERYBODY'S LOOKING FOR YOU. SECOND MOST WANTED PERSON ON EARTH. 'CAUSE REALLY, DE—NO ONE GIVES A SHIT ABOUT YOU.
WE ALL WANT HER.
WHY CAN'T YOU PEOPLE JUST LEAVE US ALONE?

THEY WANT HER. THEY ALL DO.
THEY WANT HER BLOOD. ALL OF IT. EVERY DROP.
AND I'LL KILL ANYONE WHO TRIES TO TAKE IT.
ANYONE.
BOOOOM
OOF!
CHICK? GOD. NO...
GIVE ME THE GIRL.
RIGHT NOW.
OR I'LL KILL YOU.

ART BY **ALEX SANCHEZ** COLORS BY **JAY FOTOS**

THIS WAS A SURPRISE.
A NICE ONE. CONSIDERING THAT THE LAST TIME WE STARTED A DAY LIKE THIS ENDED WITH US DAMN NEAR SHOOTING EACH OTHER.
DAY'S YOUNG. TRY NOT TO PISS ME OFF.
DEFINITELY NOT MY INTENTION.

WHEN THINGS FELL APART BACK THEN... I DOUBTED YOU. LOST FAITH IN YOU.
I'LL NEVER DO THAT AGAIN.
YOU CAN TRUST ME. ALWAYS.
THE DEATH TOLL CONTINUES TO MOUNT IN WHAT SOME ARE CALLING THE **WORST EPIDEMIC** SINCE THE **SPANISH FLU OF 1918**.

EXCEPT THIS TIME IT ISN'T A SINGLE STRAIN OF INFLUENZA, BUT DOZENS OF DISEASES THAT ARE PRESENTING AS ULTRA-AGGRESSIVE NEW STRAINS.
THESE PATHOGENS INCLUDE COMMUNICABLE STRAINS OF GENETIC DISEASES SUCH AS SICKLE CELL AND TAY SACHS. SOMETHING DOCTORS ONCE BELIEVED WAS IMPOSSIBLE.
DEVICES LIKE THIS HAVE BEEN RECOVERED NEAR FIVE SEPARATE OUTBREAK SITES.
DR. MOSES KATZ OF THE GRASSROOTS RESISTANCE GROUP PANDEMICA SAYS THAT THESE ARE "PURITY BOMBS", SO-CALLED BECAUSE THEY ARE USED TO DELIVER DESIGNER BIOWEAPONS FOR ETHNIC CLEANSING.
WHILE WHITE HOUSE OFFICIALS FLATLY DENY THAT THE RECENT OUTBREAKS ARE ANYTHING MORE THAN RADICAL NATURAL MUTATIONS, DR. KATZ SAYS THE EVIDENCE IS THERE.
HE CLAIMS THAT EVIDENCE IS BEING IGNORED OR DISMISSED AS "FAKE SCIENCE" BY THE PEOPLE IN POWER WHOSE JOB IT IS TO PROTECT AMERICAN CITIZENS.
WHAT LENDS WEIGHT TO DR. KATZ'S CLAIMS IS THE DISPROPORTIONATELY HIGH PERCENTAGE OF INFECTION AMONG PEOPLE OF COLOR.
A SENIOR WHITE HOUSE OFFICIAL REBUFFED THESE COMMENTS AND INDICATED THAT INFECTIONS ARE MERELY HIGHER IN "UNKEMPT AND UNSANITARY NEIGHBORHOODS"...
...RESULTING IN A SOCIAL MEDIA TSUNAMI OF ANGER AGAINST THIS ADMINISTRATION. #REMOVECONGRESS AND #USGENOCIDE HAVE BEEN TRENDING.
COMMUNITY LEADERS HAVE REACHED OUT TO STATE AND FEDERAL GOVERNMENT AGENCIES FOR ASSISTANCE.
AT THIS POINT, THE QUESTIONS EVERYONE NEEDS ANSWERS TO ARE—"WHAT IS REALLY HAPPENING?" AND "WHO IS GOING TO HELP?"
WHO INDEED?

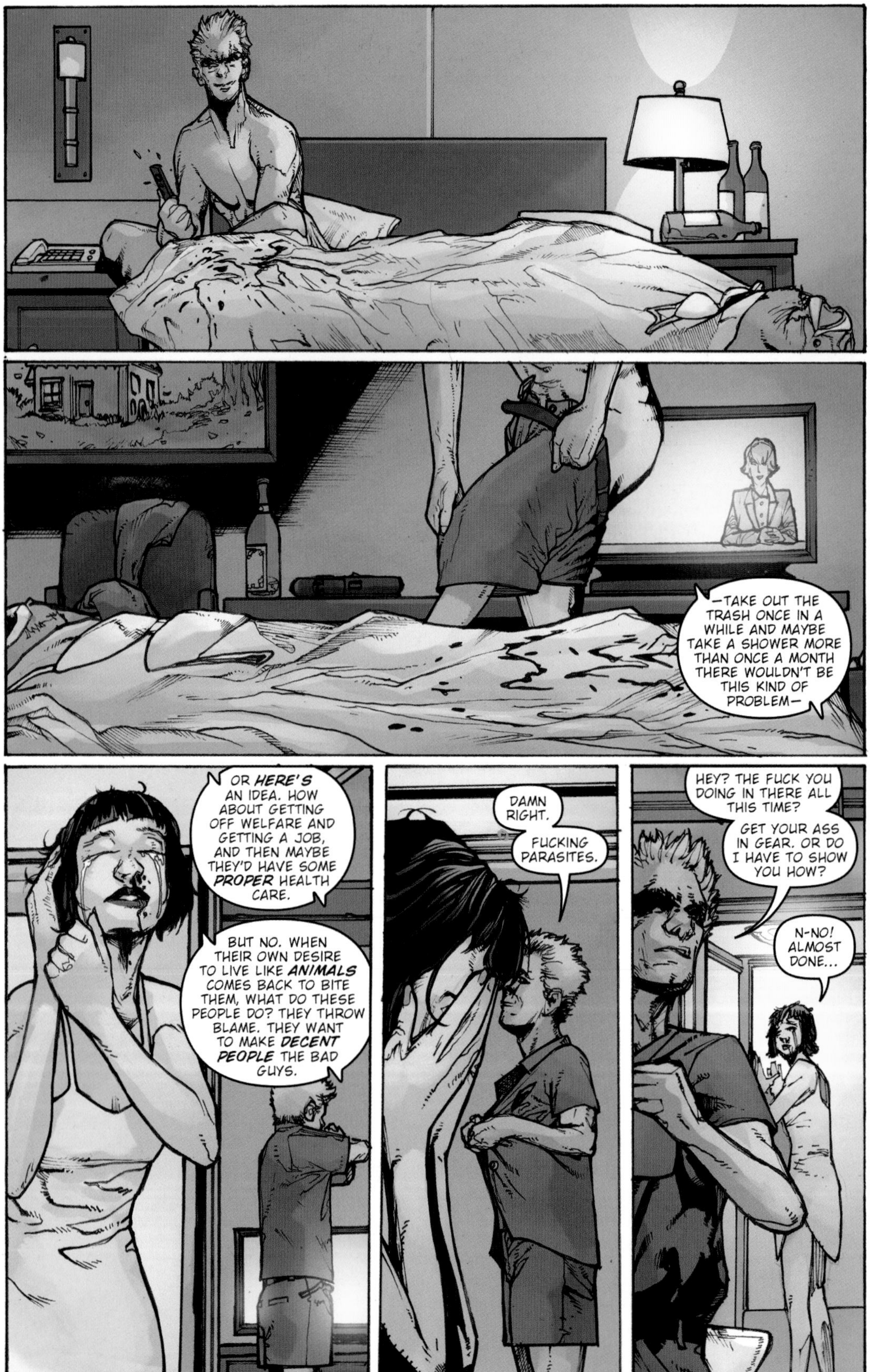
—TAKE OUT THE TRASH ONCE IN A WHILE AND MAYBE TAKE A SHOWER MORE THAN ONCE A MONTH THERE WOULDN'T BE THIS KIND OF PROBLEM—
OR HERE'S AN IDEA. HOW ABOUT GETTING OFF WELFARE AND GETTING A JOB, AND THEN MAYBE THEY'D HAVE SOME PROPER HEALTH CARE.
BUT NO. WHEN THEIR OWN DESIRE TO LIVE LIKE ANIMALS COMES BACK TO BITE THEM, WHAT DO THESE PEOPLE DO? THEY THROW BLAME. THEY WANT TO MAKE DECENT PEOPLE THE BAD GUYS.
DAMN RIGHT.
FUCKING PARASITES.
HEY? THE FUCK YOU DOING IN THERE ALL THIS TIME?
GET YOUR ASS IN GEAR. OR DO I HAVE TO SHOW YOU HOW?
N-NO! ALMOST DONE...

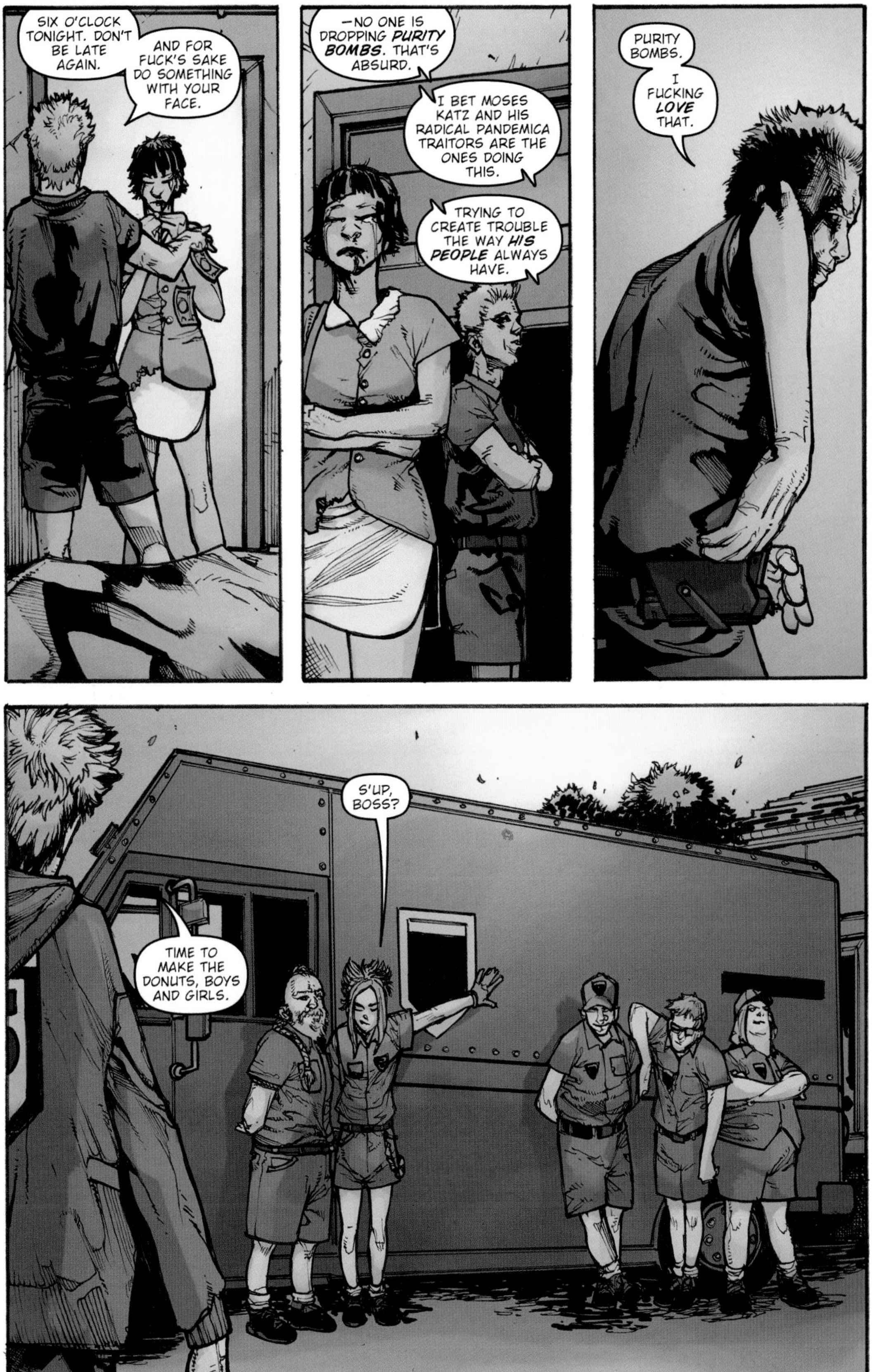
SIX O'CLOCK TONIGHT. DON'T BE LATE AGAIN.
AND FOR FUCK'S SAKE DO SOMETHING WITH YOUR FACE.
—NO ONE IS DROPPING PURITY BOMBS. THAT'S ABSURD.
I BET MOSES KATZ AND HIS RADICAL PANDEMICA TRAITORS ARE THE ONES DOING THIS.
TRYING TO CREATE TROUBLE THE WAY HIS PEOPLE ALWAYS HAVE.
PURITY BOMBS.
I FUCKING LOVE THAT.
S'UP, BOSS?
TIME TO MAKE THE DONUTS, BOYS AND GIRLS.

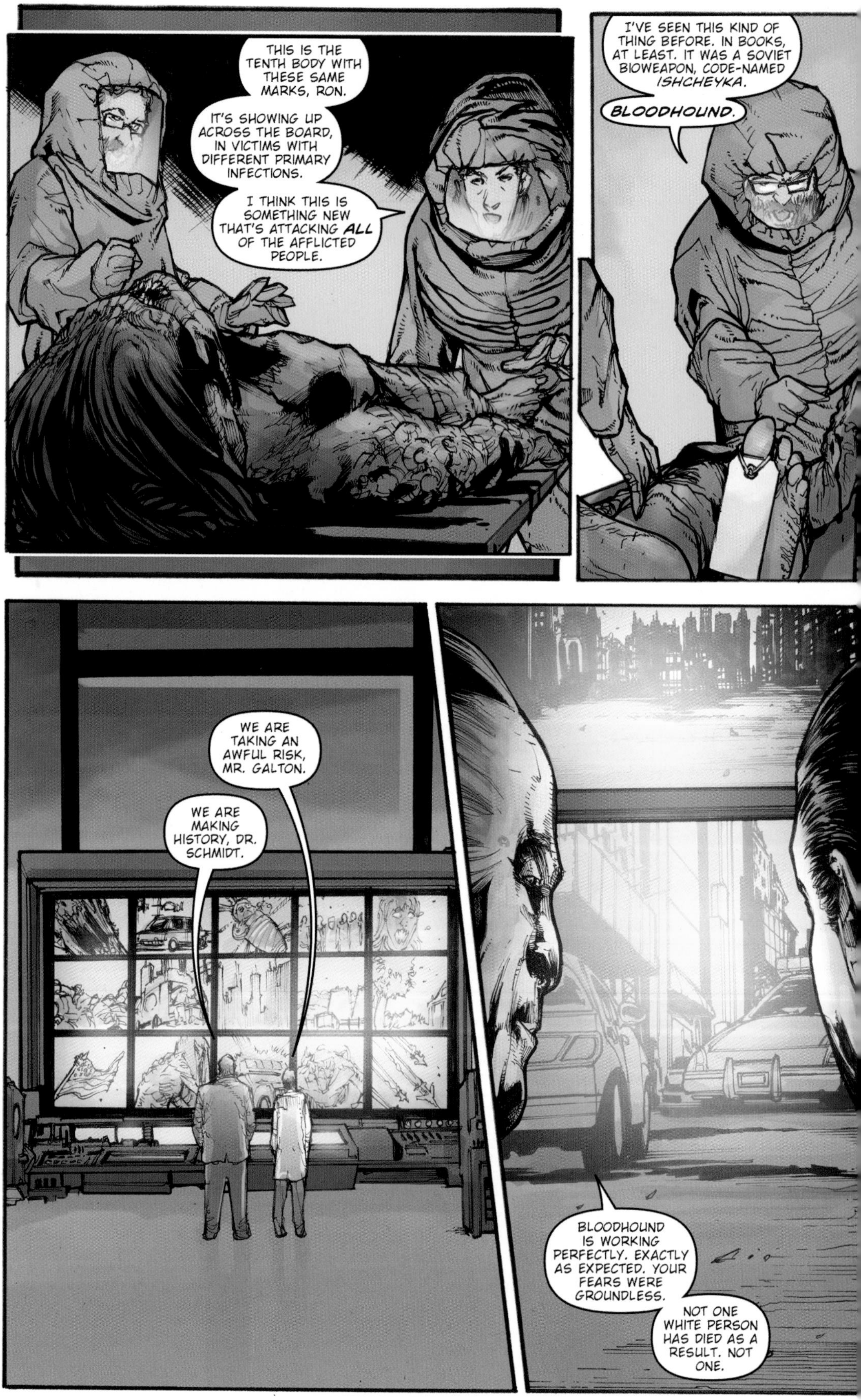
THIS IS THE TENTH BODY WITH THESE SAME MARKS, RON.
IT'S SHOWING UP ACROSS THE BOARD, IN VICTIMS WITH DIFFERENT PRIMARY INFECTIONS.
I THINK THIS IS SOMETHING NEW THAT'S ATTACKING ALL OF THE AFFLICTED PEOPLE.
I'VE SEEN THIS KIND OF THING BEFORE. IN BOOKS, AT LEAST. IT WAS A SOVIET BIOWEAPON, CODE-NAMED ISHCHEYKA.
BLOODHOUND.
WE ARE TAKING AN AWFUL RISK, MR. GALTON.
WE ARE MAKING HISTORY, DR. SCHMIDT.
BLOODHOUND IS WORKING PERFECTLY. EXACTLY AS EXPECTED. YOUR FEARS WERE GROUNDLESS.
NOT ONE WHITE PERSON HAS DIED AS A RESULT. NOT ONE.

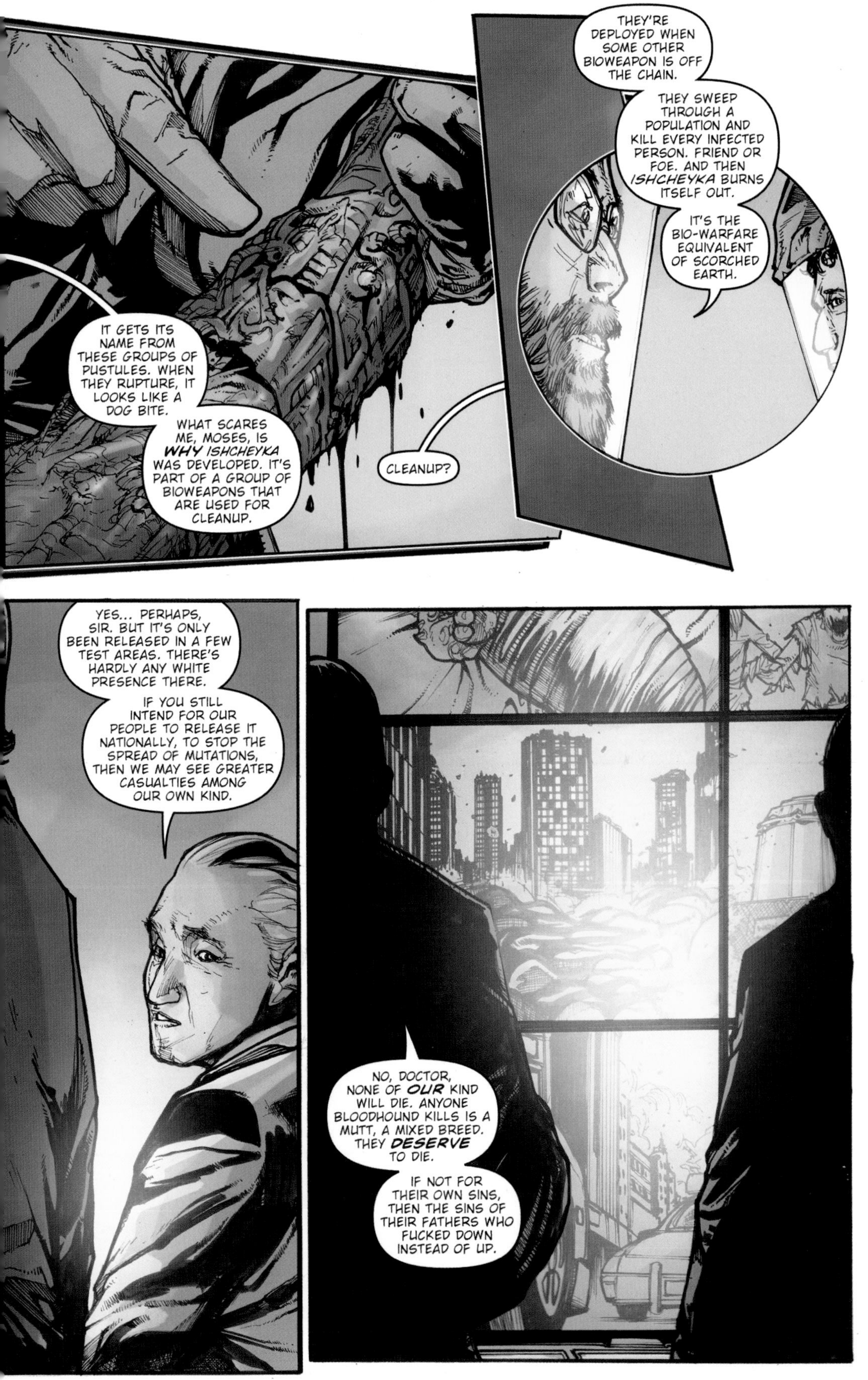
IT GETS ITS NAME FROM THESE GROUPS OF PUSTULES. WHEN THEY RUPTURE, IT LOOKS LIKE A DOG BITE.
WHAT SCARES ME, MOSES, IS WHY ISHCHEYKA WAS DEVELOPED. IT'S PART OF A GROUP OF BIOWEAPONS THAT ARE USED FOR CLEANUP.
CLEANUP?
THEY'RE DEPLOYED WHEN SOME OTHER BIOWEAPON IS OFF THE CHAIN.
THEY SWEEP THROUGH A POPULATION AND KILL EVERY INFECTED PERSON. FRIEND OR FOE. AND THEN ISHCHEYKA BURNS ITSELF OUT.
IT'S THE BIO-WARFARE EQUIVALENT OF SCORCHED EARTH.
YES... PERHAPS, SIR. BUT IT'S ONLY BEEN RELEASED IN A FEW TEST AREAS. THERE'S HARDLY ANY WHITE PRESENCE THERE.
IF YOU STILL INTEND FOR OUR PEOPLE TO RELEASE IT NATIONALLY, TO STOP THE SPREAD OF MUTATIONS, THEN WE MAY SEE GREATER CASUALTIES AMONG OUR OWN KIND.
NO, DOCTOR, NONE OF OUR KIND WILL DIE. ANYONE BLOODHOUND KILLS IS A MUTT, A MIXED BREED. THEY DESERVE TO DIE.
IF NOT FOR THEIR OWN SINS, THEN THE SINS OF THEIR FATHERS WHO FUCKED DOWN INSTEAD OF UP.

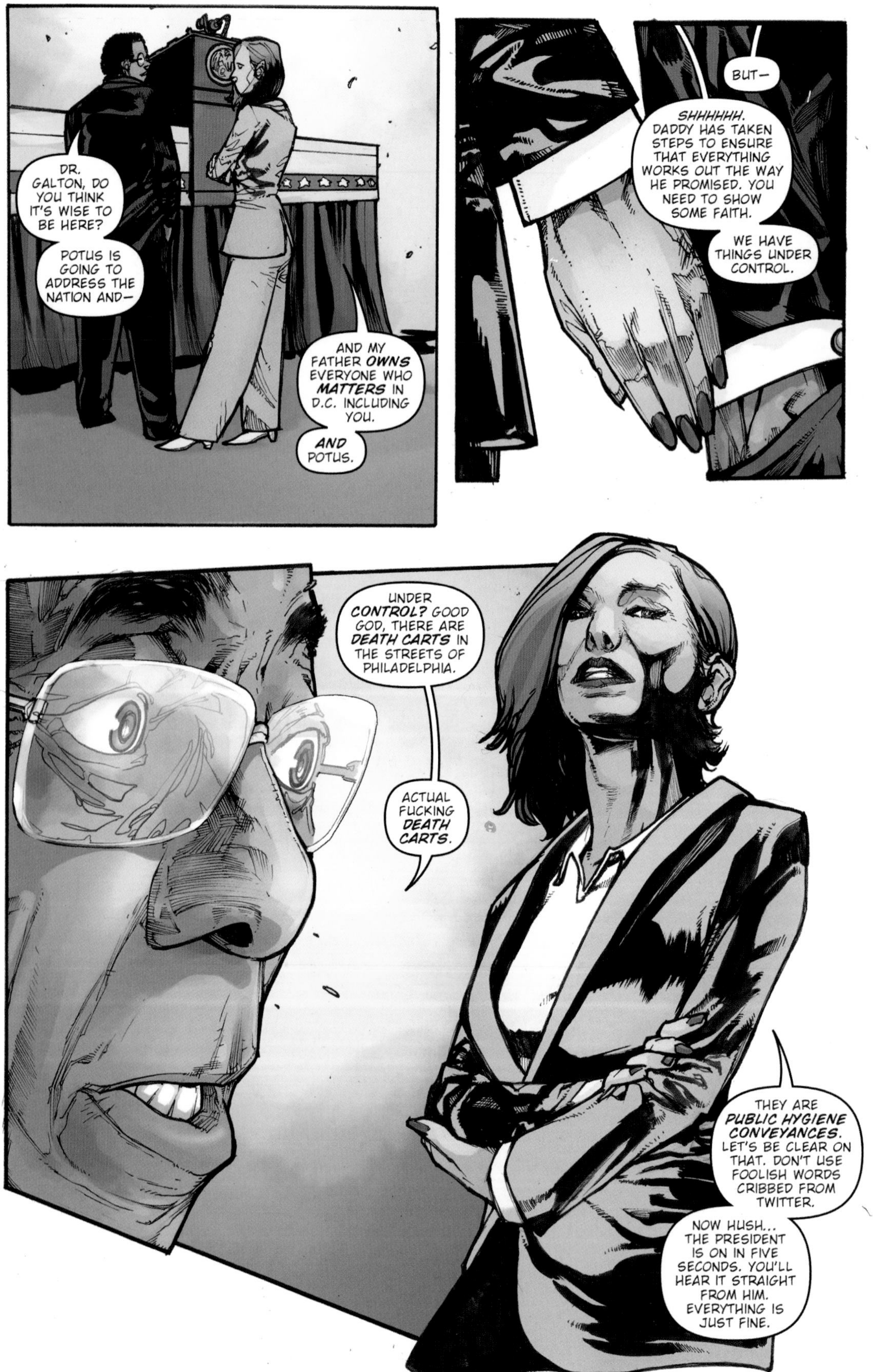
DR. GALTON, DO YOU THINK IT'S WISE TO BE HERE?
POTUS IS GOING TO ADDRESS THE NATION AND—
AND MY FATHER **OWNS** EVERYONE WHO **MATTERS** IN D.C. INCLUDING YOU.
AND POTUS.
BUT—
SHHHHHH. DADDY HAS TAKEN STEPS TO ENSURE THAT EVERYTHING WORKS OUT THE WAY HE PROMISED. YOU NEED TO SHOW SOME FAITH.
WE HAVE THINGS UNDER CONTROL.
UNDER ***CONTROL?*** GOOD GOD, THERE ARE ***DEATH CARTS*** IN THE STREETS OF PHILADELPHIA.
ACTUAL FUCKING ***DEATH CARTS***.
THEY ARE ***PUBLIC HYGIENE CONVEYANCES***. LET'S BE CLEAR ON THAT. DON'T USE FOOLISH WORDS CRIBBED FROM TWITTER.
NOW HUSH... THE PRESIDENT IS ON IN FIVE SECONDS. YOU'LL HEAR IT STRAIGHT FROM HIM. EVERYTHING IS JUST FINE.

—ASSURE YOU, MY FELLOW AMERICANS, THAT THERE IS NO CRISIS.
THE FAKE NEWS IS GLUTTED WITH FAKE SCIENCE. REPORTS OF MUTATIONS AND MASS DEATHS ARE GREATLY EXAGGERATED.
WHITMAN LABORATORIES
AMERICA HAS THE GREATEST MEDICAL COVERAGE IN THE WORLD. YES, THIS IS A CONCERN, BUT IT IS NOT A CRISIS.
YOU COULD HAVE FERTILIZED A FOUR ACRE BEANFIELD WITH ALL THAT BULLSHIT.
WHAT IS IT WITH POLITICIANS ANYMORE? THEY EITHER HAVE THEIR HEADS SO FAR UP THEIR OWN ASSES THEY CAN'T HEAR OR SEE WHAT'S GOING ON OR THEY DON'T GIVE A COLD SHIT ABOUT PEOPLE.
THEY'RE OWNED BY WHOEVER PAID FOR THEIR CAMPAIGNS.
THEY'VE BEEN LOOKING THE OTHER WAY WHILE THE CLIMATE GOES TO HELL.
WHY WOULD YOU THINK IT'S ANY DIFFERENT WHEN SOMEONE STARTS KILLING OFF INCONVENIENT PEOPLE?
TELL YOU WHAT, DE—I AIN'T BEEN CARRYING AROUND MUCH EXTRA OPTIMISM LATELY. NOT WHILE RUNNING DOWN BAD GUYS FOR THE U.N. AND W.H.O. AND SURE AS FUCK NOT SINCE SIGNING ON WITH YOU AND MOSES.
LOOK, CHICK, WE'VE BROKEN ABOUT A THOUSAND LAWS SO FAR AND COULD RIDE THE NEEDLE FOR WHAT WE'RE DOING. IF YOU NEED TO STEP BACK FROM THIS—
OH, HUSH NOW, WOMAN. I SIGNED ON FOR THE WHOLE RIDE.
TRUTH IS, DE, I'VE DONE WORSE THINGS FOR WORSE CAUSES. HELL, I'VE EVEN BEEN A KIND OF BAD GUY TIME AND AGAIN.
NATURE OF SPECOPS AND MORE SO OF BEING A PRIVATE MILITARY CONTRACTOR. NOT A LOT OF WHITE HATS.
BUT THIS? HELL, THIS IS ILLEGAL AS FUCK. IT'S MASS MURDER AND CAPITAL CRIME.
BUT FOR ONCE I KNOW—ABSOLUTELY KNOW—I'M ON THE SIDE OF THE ANGELS.

I AGREE, DR. KATZ. WE CAN'T LET THIS CONTINUE.
AND YOU SAY THAT OTHER SENATORS WILL STEP UP? HOW MANY?
ENOUGH, I HOPE. BOTH SIDES OF THE AISLE. BUT WE NEED PROOF.
AND YOU'LL HAVE IT. MY PEOPLE ARE PUTTING TOGETHER A PRESENTATION THAT WILL PROVE—PROVE—WHAT I'VE BEEN SAYING.
I'VE GOT LAB REPORTS COMING IN TODAY FROM SIX SEPARATE INDEPENDENT LABS. YOU LINE UP YOUR PEOPLE, AND I'LL GIVE YOU ALL THE AMMUNITION YOU'LL NEED.
DOC, THE DELIVERY GUYS ARE HERE. I BUZZED THEM UP.
OUT-FUCKING-STANDING.
I APPRECIATE THE TRUST YOU'RE SHOWING HERE, SENATOR. AND THE GENUINE PATRIOTISM.
HEH, HEH... MAKES ME WISH I'D VOTED FOR YOU IN THE LAST ELECTION.
SPECIAL DELIVERY.

THERE ARE A LOT OF WAYS TO DO THIS.
STEALTH WORKS MOST OF THE TIME.
EXCEPT WHEN IT DOESN'T.
OR WHEN YOU DON'T GIVE ENOUGH OF A FUCK TO BE SNEAKY.
CASE IN POINT.
SURVIVORS ARE POTENTIAL WITNESSES. WE DON'T NEED THAT KIND OF COMPLICATION.

GOD! YOU'RE THOSE PANDEMICA MANIACS!
YOU REALLY THINK THIS IS A GOOD NAME CALLING MOMENT, HOSS?
YOU'RE WELL AND TRULY FUCKED RIGHT NOW. I GOT A SPARE BULLET, AND UNLESS YOU HAVE SOMETHING TO TRADE...
CHRIST, NO! LISTEN... LISTEN... *FUCK THIS HURTS...*
GUT SHOTS TEND TO. WE CAN GET YOU TO AN ER, HAVE THEM FIX YOU UP SO YOU WON'T SHIT IN A BAG THE REST OF YOUR LIFE. BUT YOU HAVE TO EARN IT.
LISTEN TO ME—I'M A LAB DRONE. I JUST WORK FOR THEM.
WORK FOR *WHO*, EXACTLY? NAMES.
JENN SOMETHING AND HER FATHER. I DON'T KNOW LAST NAMES.
YOU'RE NOT BEING USEFUL.
WAIT! YOU WANT NAMES?
I CAN'T GIVE YOU ANY, BUT I CAN GIVE YOU SOMETHING BETTER.
I CAN GIVE YOU A PATHWAY TO A CURE.
TO WHICH DISEASE?
WHY... TO *ALL* OF THEM. IT'S DOWNSTAIRS. DOWN WHERE THEY KEEP THE BABIES.
BABIES...
FUCK ME.

WELL, IF IT ISN'T THE KING OF THE JEWS.
NO, WAIT, THAT WAS JESUS. AND I DON'T THINK YOU HAVE THE POWER TO COME BACK FROM THE DEAD.
OR DO YOU WANT TO TEST THAT? NO? GOOD. NOW, TELL ME WHERE THE FUCK I CAN FIND DE'NEESA AND CHICK.
I'M REALLY ITCHING TO SHOOT THE SHIT WITH MY OLD ROAD DOGS.
WHO? I... I DON'T KNOW THEM.
NEVER HEARD OF ANYONE BY THOSE NAMES.
YOU SURE ABOUT THAT?
NO! YOU'RE MAKING A TERRIBLE MISTAKE.
I DON'T MAKE MISTAKES, JEWBOY.
BANG

LISTEN TO ME, JEWBOY. DE AND CHICK KILLED A WHOLE BUNCH OF MY PEOPLE.
I ONLY TOOK ONE OF YOURS.
BUT, TELL YOU WHAT...
YOU HAVE TWENTY-FOUR HOURS TO GET MY TWO OLD DANCING PARTNERS TO TURN THEMSELVES OVER TO ME. THEM AND ALL THE INFO THEY STOLE FROM MY BOSS.
THEY DO THAT, AND NO ONE ELSE HERE HAS TO DIE.
THAT'S ME BEING A NICE GUY. I WANT DE'NEESA AND CHICK AT THIS ADDRESS BY TOMORROW NOON.
OTHERWISE, EVERYONE HERE—AND EVERYONE THEY LOVE, ALL THE WAY DOWN TO TIT-SUCKING BABIES AND THE FAMILY DOG—GO OUT HARD.
YA'LL HAVE A REAL NICE DAY, NOW.

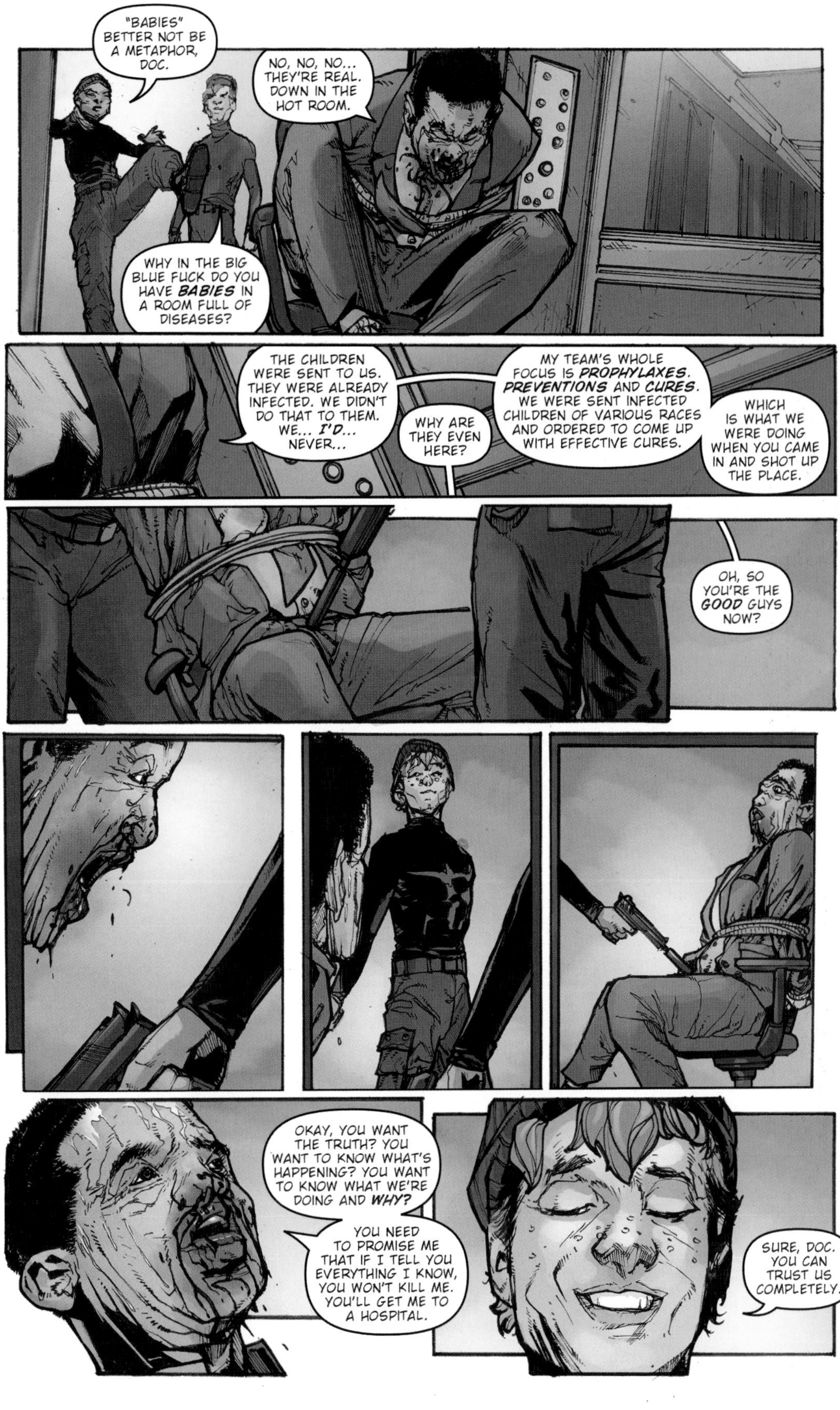
"BABIES" BETTER NOT BE A METAPHOR, DOC.
NO, NO, NO... THEY'RE REAL. DOWN IN THE HOT ROOM.
WHY IN THE BIG BLUE FUCK DO YOU HAVE **BABIES** IN A ROOM FULL OF DISEASES?
THE CHILDREN WERE SENT TO US. THEY WERE ALREADY INFECTED. WE DIDN'T DO THAT TO THEM. WE... **I'D**... NEVER...
WHY ARE THEY EVEN HERE?
MY TEAM'S WHOLE FOCUS IS **PROPHYLAXES. PREVENTIONS** AND **CURES**. WE WERE SENT INFECTED CHILDREN OF VARIOUS RACES AND ORDERED TO COME UP WITH EFFECTIVE CURES.
WHICH IS WHAT WE WERE DOING WHEN YOU CAME IN AND SHOT UP THE PLACE.
OH, SO YOU'RE THE **GOOD** GUYS NOW?
OKAY, YOU WANT THE TRUTH? YOU WANT TO KNOW WHAT'S HAPPENING? YOU WANT TO KNOW WHAT WE'RE DOING AND **WHY?**
YOU NEED TO PROMISE ME THAT IF I TELL YOU EVERYTHING I KNOW, YOU WON'T KILL ME. YOU'LL GET ME TO A HOSPITAL.
SURE, DOC. YOU CAN TRUST US COMPLETELY.

DR. KATZ HAS BEEN ON ALL THE NEWS SERVICES YELLING ABOUT ETHNIC GENOCIDE. OKAY, FINE. HE'S NOT WRONG. IT'S NOT A CONSPIRACY THEORY. IT'S FACT.
THE GOAL OF ARK IS TO CULL THE HUMAN HERD BY REDUCING THE NUMBER OF UNDESIRABLE PEOPLES. PEOPLE WHO TAKE AND DON'T GIVE BACK.
THE ACCIDENTS OF EVOLUTION.
RESETTING THE NATURAL ORDER SO THAT THE ARYAN RACE—GOD'S *ACTUAL* CHOSEN PEOPLE—CAN RECLAIM THEIR RIGHTFUL PLACE.
THAT'S WHAT WE WERE ALL SOLD ON. ME, TOO. I ADMIT IT.
TEAMS HAVE COLLECTED ETHNIC-SPECIFIC BIOWEAPONS FROM AROUND THE WORLD. DOZENS OF LABS WERE SET UP AND PRIVATELY FUNDED.
WE USED CRISPR GENE-EDITING TECHNOLOGY AND OTHER METHODS TO REFINE AND PERFECT THOSE OLD WEAPONS. AND WE BUILT MANY NEW ONES. VERY TARGETED.
ARK SOLD MANY OF THESE WEAPONS FOR LIMITED USE BY CERTAIN POLITICAL GROUPS. THEY NEEDED A RIVAL ETHNICITY ELIMINATED AND WERE WILLING TO PAY FOR IT.
THAT MONEY FUNDED A DEEPER LEVEL OF RESEARCH.
THE GOAL IS TO CHANGE THE POPULATION DEMOGRAPHICS SO THAT THE WHITE RACE IS DOMINANT ONCE AGAIN. AMERICA FIRST, THEN ELSEWHERE.
HELL... WITH SO MANY MUD PEOPLE GONE, THERE WILL BE FEWER CARS, FEWER HERDS OF FARTING COWS, FEWER POLLUTANTS FROM FACTORIES.
WE'LL SAVE THE RACE *AND* SOLVE CLIMATE CHANGE, ALL AT ONCE.
PING

MBWIRI
ERES
KEK
MYA
GRAY DRAGON
TOTEM
ALGHUL
TRICKSTER
TENGU
HARVESTER

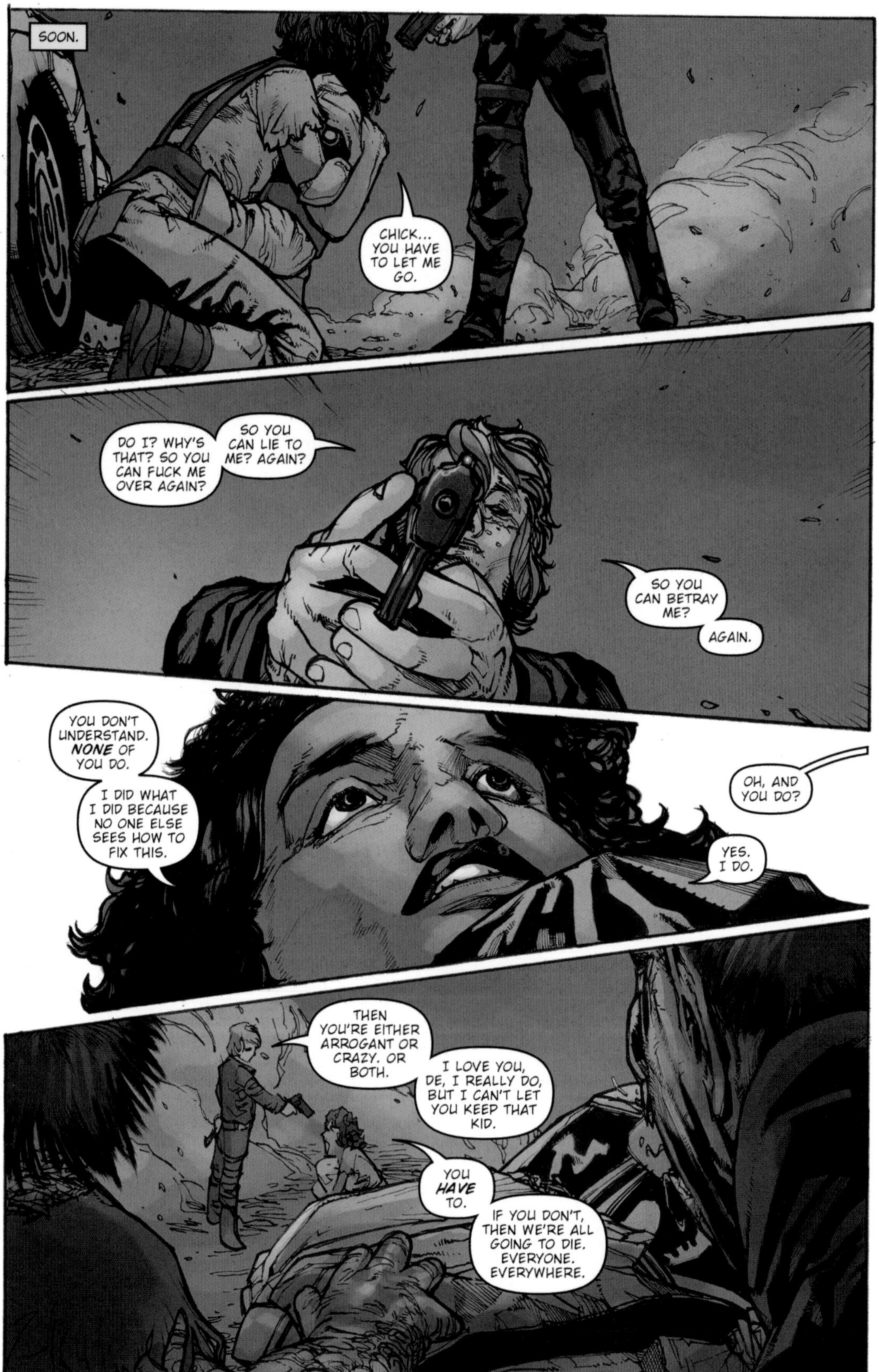
SOON.
CHICK... YOU HAVE TO LET ME GO.
DO I? WHY'S THAT? SO YOU CAN FUCK ME OVER AGAIN?
SO YOU CAN LIE TO ME? AGAIN?
SO YOU CAN BETRAY ME?
AGAIN.
YOU DON'T UNDERSTAND. ***NONE*** OF YOU DO.
I DID WHAT I DID BECAUSE NO ONE ELSE SEES HOW TO FIX THIS.
OH, AND YOU DO?
YES. I DO.
THEN YOU'RE EITHER ARROGANT OR CRAZY. OR BOTH.
I LOVE YOU, DE, I REALLY DO, BUT I CAN'T LET YOU KEEP THAT KID.
YOU ***HAVE*** TO.
IF YOU DON'T, THEN WE'RE ALL GOING TO DIE. EVERYONE. EVERYWHERE.

BECAUSE YOU KNOW HOW THIS ENDS WHEN NO ONE ELSE DOES?
GOD DAMN, YOU CAN'T HELP BUT BREAK MY HEART.
IF YOU LOVE ME—IF YOU EVER LOVED ME—TRUST ME NOW. I NEED TO FIND THE LIGHTHOUSE.
JESUS FUCK, DE, THERE IS NO LIGHTHOUSE. IT'S A MYTH. IT'S WHAT DESPERATE PEOPLE TELL EACH OTHER BECAUSE THEY'RE TOO STUPID TO REALIZE THE WORLD HAS GONE TO SHIT.
AND THAT KID YOU'RE CARRYING IS LIKE AN ATOM BOMB. LIKE A MILLION ATOM BOMBS. THE ONLY THING KEEPING WHAT'S LEFT OF THE WORLD ALIVE IS THAT HAZMAT SUIT.
CHICK... YOU TOLD ME ONCE THAT I COULD TRUST YOU. DO YOU REMEMBER?
THAT MORNING WHEN WE MADE LOVE BEFORE WE HIT THAT LAB?
YOU SWORE TO ME THAT I COULD ALWAYS TRUST YOU.
I'M TRUSTING YOU NOW. I'M GOING TO TURN AND WALK AWAY.
I DON'T THINK YOU'RE GOING TO SHOOT ME. I DON'T THINK YOU'RE GOING TO SHOOT THE BABY.
JESUS CHRIST, DE...

DON'T MAKE ME WRONG ABOUT THIS.

POKA-
POKA-
POKA-
POKA-

ART BY **ALEX SANCHEZ** COLORS BY **JAY FOTOS**

JUST WHEN YOU THINK YOU'VE SEEN IT ALL.
JUST WHEN YOU THINK THE WORLD COULD NOT GET ANY COLDER.
ANY UGLIER.
THE WORLD LOVES TO PROVE YOU WRONG.
TO SHOW YOU HOW NAIVE YOU ARE.
THINGS CAN *ALWAYS* GET WORSE.
MUCH, *MUCH* WORSE.

LOOK, I CAN ACTUALLY SEE YOUR BLEEDING HEART DRIPPING ALL OVER THE FLOOR. SURE. I GET IT. I'M NOT ACTUALLY HEARTLESS.
IF YOU WANT TO BE HEROES AND SAVE SOME KIDS, THEN TAKE THOSE.
WHY THEM AND NOT ALL OF THE KIDS?
BECAUSE THEY AREN'T INFECTED. THEY'RE HERE FOR IMMUNIZATION TRIALS.
ALL OF THOSE OTHER KIDS ARE HIGHLY INFECTIOUS. TAKE THEM OUT OF CONTAINMENT AND I GUARANTEE THAT YOU'LL BE DOING MORE HARM THAN GOOD.
WHAT ABOUT HER?
GOD! DON'T YOU DARE.
YOU DON'T WANT TO BE TELLING US WHAT WE DO AND DON'T DARE.
SURE. FINE. TAKE HER. AND KILL EVERY FUCKING THING THAT LIVES ON THIS PLANET...
WHAT ARE YOU TALKING ABOUT?

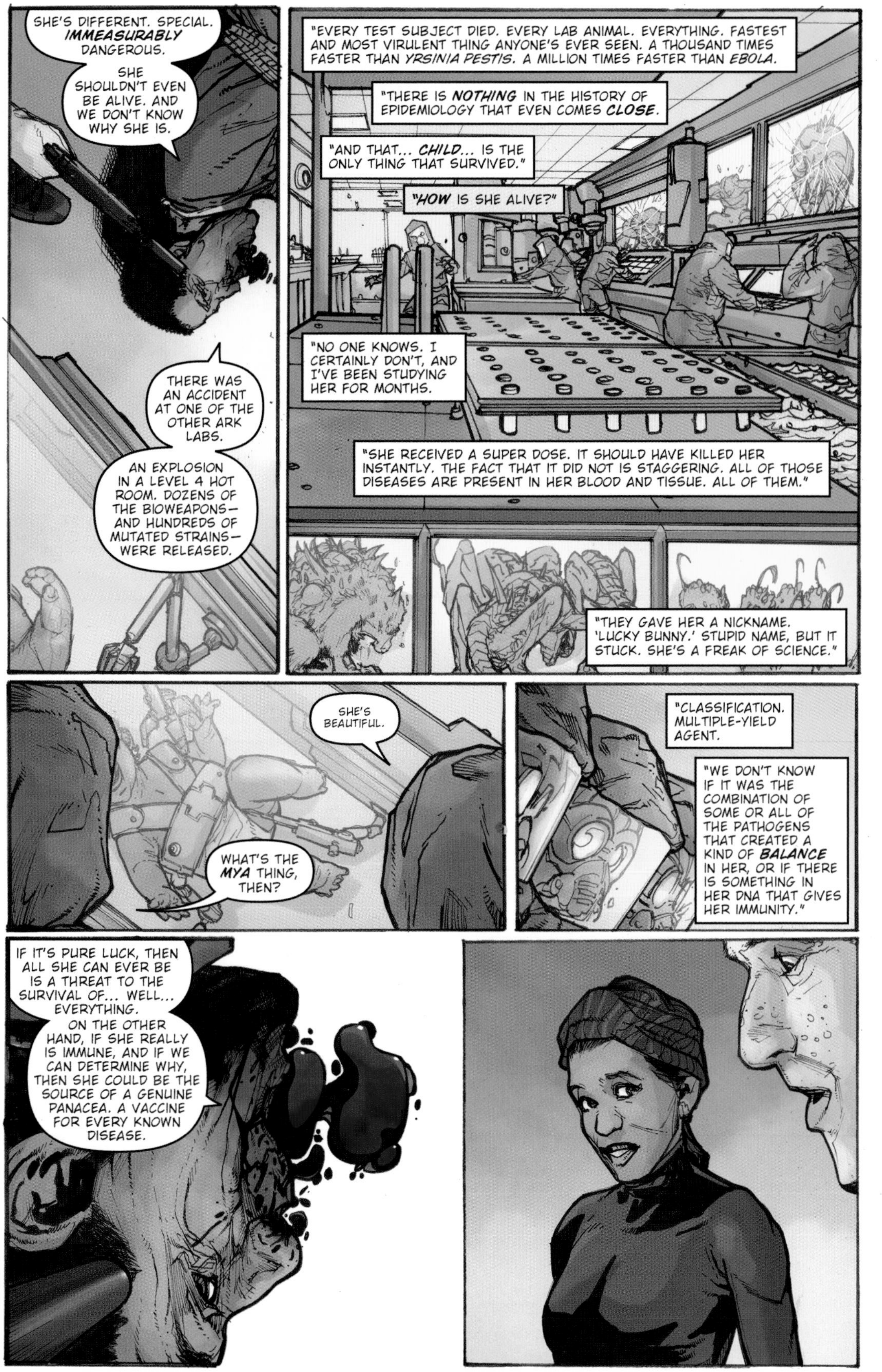

SHE'S DIFFERENT. SPECIAL. IMMEASURABLY DANGEROUS.
SHE SHOULDN'T EVEN BE ALIVE. AND WE DON'T KNOW WHY SHE IS.
THERE WAS AN ACCIDENT AT ONE OF THE OTHER ARK LABS.
AN EXPLOSION IN A LEVEL 4 HOT ROOM. DOZENS OF THE BIOWEAPONS—AND HUNDREDS OF MUTATED STRAINS—WERE RELEASED.
"EVERY TEST SUBJECT DIED. EVERY LAB ANIMAL. EVERYTHING. FASTEST AND MOST VIRULENT THING ANYONE'S EVER SEEN. A THOUSAND TIMES FASTER THAN YRSINIA PESTIS. A MILLION TIMES FASTER THAN EBOLA.
"THERE IS NOTHING IN THE HISTORY OF EPIDEMIOLOGY THAT EVEN COMES CLOSE.
"AND THAT... CHILD... IS THE ONLY THING THAT SURVIVED."
"HOW IS SHE ALIVE?"
"NO ONE KNOWS. I CERTAINLY DON'T, AND I'VE BEEN STUDYING HER FOR MONTHS.
"SHE RECEIVED A SUPER DOSE. IT SHOULD HAVE KILLED HER INSTANTLY. THE FACT THAT IT DID NOT IS STAGGERING. ALL OF THOSE DISEASES ARE PRESENT IN HER BLOOD AND TISSUE. ALL OF THEM."
"THEY GAVE HER A NICKNAME. 'LUCKY BUNNY.' STUPID NAME, BUT IT STUCK. SHE'S A FREAK OF SCIENCE."
SHE'S BEAUTIFUL.
WHAT'S THE MYA THING, THEN?
"CLASSIFICATION. MULTIPLE-YIELD AGENT.
"WE DON'T KNOW IF IT WAS THE COMBINATION OF SOME OR ALL OF THE PATHOGENS THAT CREATED A KIND OF BALANCE IN HER, OR IF THERE IS SOMETHING IN HER DNA THAT GIVES HER IMMUNITY."
IF IT'S PURE LUCK, THEN ALL SHE CAN EVER BE IS A THREAT TO THE SURVIVAL OF... WELL... EVERYTHING.
ON THE OTHER HAND, IF SHE REALLY IS IMMUNE, AND IF WE CAN DETERMINE WHY, THEN SHE COULD BE THE SOURCE OF A GENUINE PANACEA. A VACCINE FOR EVERY KNOWN DISEASE.

HOW ALL THESE PATHOGENS ACHIEVED A KIND OF STASIS IN LUCKY BUNNY'S TISSUE IS BEYOND UNDERSTANDING...
I SAW THIS GIRL BEFORE.
NOT THE SAME CHILD, BUT SOMEONE LIKE HER.
GOD IN HEAVEN...
DEMOCRATIC REPUBLIC OF CONGO.
IT'S DENGUE FEVER. YOU WERE ALMOST RIGHT ABOUT THAT. BUT THIS CHILD HAS DENGUE HEMORRHAGIC FEVER.
SHE'S WELL INTO DENGUE SHOCK SYNDROME.
I KNOW YOU WERE TRYING TO SAVE HER. BUT YOU BROKE PROTOCOLS BY BRINGING HER HERE.
IT BREAKS MY HEART TO SAY IT, BUT YOU SHOULD HAVE LET HER DIE IN HER VILLAGE.
GOD IN HEAVEN...

...BUNNY IS VERY SPECIAL. HER DNA SHOWS THE MOST COMPLETE MIX OF HUMAN RACIAL GENES HE'S EVER SEEN.
WE CAN CURE SOME OF THE DISEASES SHE HAS, BUT FRANKLY, WE'RE AFRAID TO. THERE SEEMS TO BE A BALANCE, AND ANY CHANGE MIGHT KILL HER. OR MAKE THE DISEASE CLUSTER SPIRAL OUT OF CONTROL.
ARK WANTED HER KILLED BECAUSE SHE REPRESENTS THE FUTURE OF EARTH—TOTAL MIXED RACES. THE POLLUTED EVE OF A POLLUTED EDEN.
BUT WE DOCTORS KEPT HER ALIVE BECAUSE OF HER UNIQUE RESISTANCE.
AND NOW YOU'VE DESTROYED EVERYTHING WE'VE WORKED FOR.
DUDE, YOU'RE AN ACTUAL MAD SCIENTIST TRYING TO MAKE THE WORLD INTO SOMETHING IT NEVER WAS.
READ YOUR OWN SCIENTIFIC HISTORY. HUMAN LIFE STARTED IN AFRICA, AND I HATE TO BREAK IT TO YOU, BUT WE DIDN'T START OUT WHITE.
MAYBE NOT. MAYBE ARK'S PHILOSOPHY HAS SOME BUGS IN IT—BUT THEIR GOAL IS PURE. CULL THE POPULATION AND SAVE THE WORLD.
SURE, A WHITEWASHED VANILLA WORLD. ***HOO-FUCKING-RAH.***
SO, ON BEHALF THE MAJORITY OF WHITE FOLKS WHO ARE NOT RACIST ASS-FUCKS, WHY DON'T YOU SKIP THE BULLSHIT RAH-RAH EUGENICS CRAP...
...AND TELL ME HOW WE CAN GET THESE KIDS OUT OF HERE SAFELY.
YOU HAVEN'T BEEN LISTENING. ONLY THE UNINFECTED ONES CAN BE MOVED.
MAYBE THE INFECTED ONES, IF YOU HAVE AN L4 CONTAINMENT VAN. THERE'S A DOOR DOWN HERE THAT WILL TAKE YOU RIGHT TO THE UNDERGROUND GARAGE.
BUT NOT HER. GOD. NO. ***NOT HER.***
LOOK, THIS ISN'T ME—SOMEONE WORKING FOR ARK—SAYING THIS.
THIS IS SOMEONE WHO DOESN'T WANT TO SEE THE ENTIRE WORLD DIE WARNING YOU—NO, ***BEGGING*** YOU—TO NOT TOUCH HER.
I CAN INJECT SOMETHING INTO HER FEEDING TUBE. AND THEN YOU SHOULD BURN THE BODY.

ARE YOU OUT OF YOUR FUCKING MIND?
LISTEN TO ME YOU PIECE OF SHIT—THAT IS A CHILD THERE.
IT'S NOT MY FAULT. IT HAPPENED AT A DIFFERENT LAB.
IT HAPPENED AT AN ARK LAB. I'M MAKING IT YOUR FAULT.
FIND ME A WAY TO GET HER OUT OF HERE SAFELY, OR SO HELP ME GOD I WILL RUIN YOU.
WHY WON'T YOU LISTEN? SHE CAN'T BE SAVED. SHE'S TOO DANGEROUS.
SHE'S MORE DANGEROUS THAN TEN THOUSAND NUCLEAR BOMBS.
YOU CAN'T SAVE HER. ALL YOU CAN DO IS KILL EVERYONE.
LOOK, DE, I HATE TO AGREE WITH THAT PILE OF YAK SHIT, BUT MAYBE HE'S RIGHT. IF LIL' BUNNY THERE'S AS BAD AS HE SAYS, THEN WHAT HOPE IS THERE FOR HER?
WE CAN USE ONE OF THOSE TO GET HER OUT. TAKE HER SOMEWHERE SAFE.
BUT IS IT WORTH THE RISK? IF SHE'S EVEN A TENTH AS BAD AS HE'S SAYING, THEN ONE TEAR IN THE FABRIC, ONE LITTLE FUCK UP IN SAFETY PROTOCOLS, AND THE DEATHS WE'VE SEEN SO FAR WILL BE NOTHING.
DID YOU FORGET TO BRING YOUR BALLS WITH YOU TODAY, CHICK?
HEY, ANSWER THE FUCKING QUESTION—HOW IS IT WORTH THE RISK?
NO, LISTEN TO ME. SHE'S INFECTED, BUT NOT SICK. THAT'S GOLDEN. THAT'S A GIFT FROM GOD. THAT'S THE UNIVERSE CUTTING US THE ONLY BREAK WE'VE HAD SINCE THIS THING STARTED.
speaker
keypad
J. GALTON

OR IT'S THE DEVIL BENDING US OVER AND ASS-FUCKING US WHILE HE LAUGHS. NO WAY I'M TAKING THAT KID OUT OF HERE.
THEN DON'T. *I* WILL.
THE FUCK YOU WILL.
ARE YOU GOING TO STOP ME?
I WILL IF I HAVE TO, DE, BUT—FUCK, MAN—DON'T ***MAKE*** ME.
SWEET JESUS ON THE CROSS.
HASKINS, IT'S JENN—
IT'S NOT A GOOD TIME, JENN. WE HAVE NEW OUTBREAKS IN—
SHUT UP AND LISTEN. IT'S CHICK WEED AND THAT BITCH DE'NEESA. THEY'RE AT LAB 16.
THEY'RE GOING TO TRY AND TAKE THE ***BUNNY***.
NOT ON MY FUCKING WATCH.

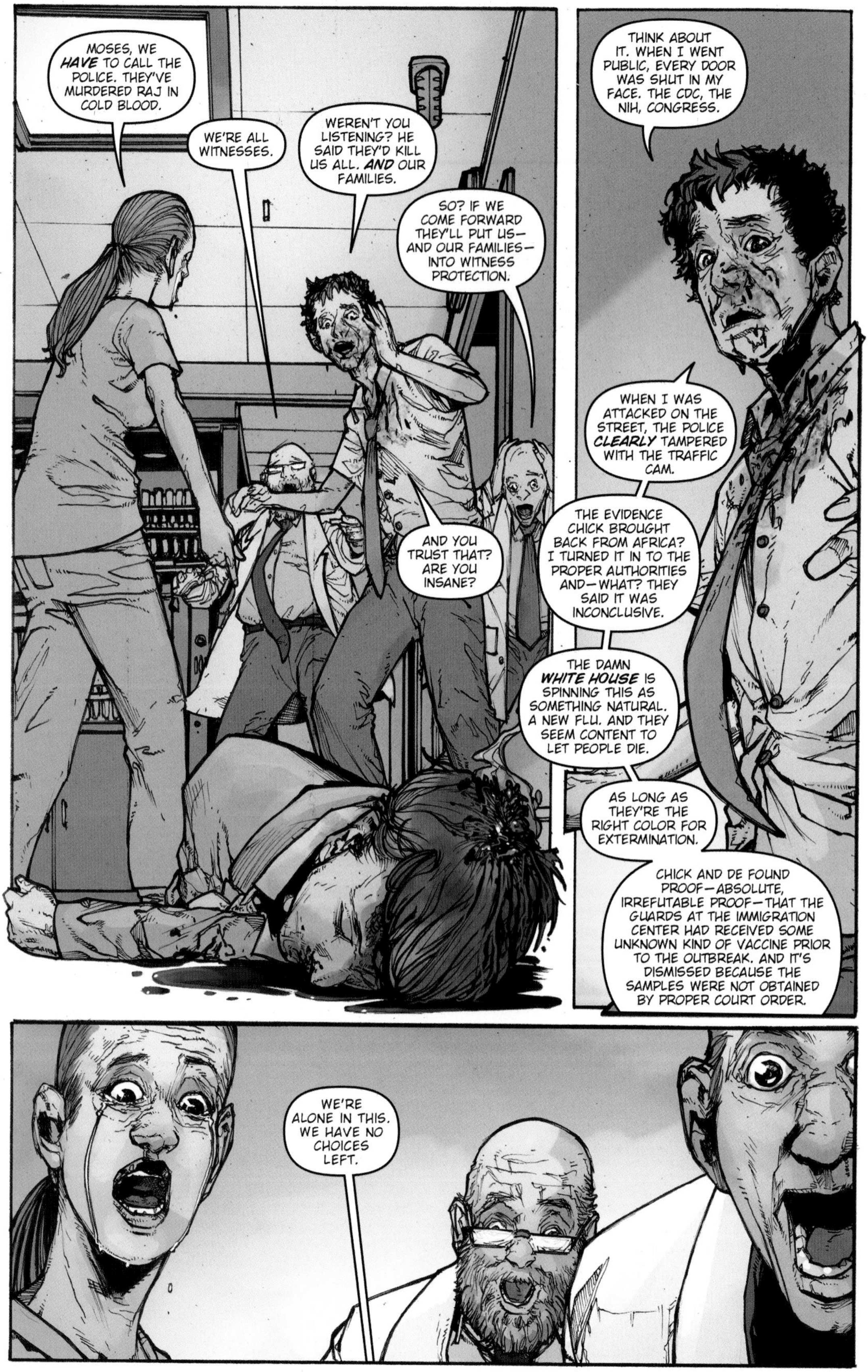
MOSES, WE *HAVE* TO CALL THE POLICE. THEY'VE MURDERED RAJ IN COLD BLOOD.
WE'RE ALL WITNESSES.
WEREN'T YOU LISTENING? HE SAID THEY'D KILL US ALL. *AND* OUR FAMILIES.
SO? IF WE COME FORWARD THEY'LL PUT US—AND OUR FAMILIES—INTO WITNESS PROTECTION.
AND YOU TRUST THAT? ARE YOU INSANE?
THINK ABOUT IT. WHEN I WENT PUBLIC, EVERY DOOR WAS SHUT IN MY FACE. THE CDC, THE NIH, CONGRESS.
WHEN I WAS ATTACKED ON THE STREET, THE POLICE *CLEARLY* TAMPERED WITH THE TRAFFIC CAM.
THE EVIDENCE CHICK BROUGHT BACK FROM AFRICA? I TURNED IT IN TO THE PROPER AUTHORITIES AND—WHAT? THEY SAID IT WAS INCONCLUSIVE.
THE DAMN *WHITE HOUSE* IS SPINNING THIS AS SOMETHING NATURAL. A NEW FLU. AND THEY SEEM CONTENT TO LET PEOPLE DIE.
AS LONG AS THEY'RE THE RIGHT COLOR FOR EXTERMINATION.
CHICK AND DE FOUND PROOF—ABSOLUTE, IRREFUTABLE PROOF—THAT THE GUARDS AT THE IMMIGRATION CENTER HAD RECEIVED SOME UNKNOWN KIND OF VACCINE PRIOR TO THE OUTBREAK. AND IT'S DISMISSED BECAUSE THE SAMPLES WERE NOT OBTAINED BY PROPER COURT ORDER.
WE'RE ALONE IN THIS. WE HAVE NO CHOICES LEFT.

NO! NO FUCKING WAY. WE'VE ALL RISKED EVERYTHING TO FIGHT THIS. OUR JOBS, OUR CREDIBILITY. FRIENDS.
PEOPLE ARE DYING BY THE THOUSANDS!
THAT'S MY NEIGHBORHOOD, MOSES. THAT KID PLAYS WITH MY KIDS. THEY GO TO THE SAME SCHOOL.
HOW CAN WE GIVE UP? THIS DISEASE IS HUNTING US—OUR FAMILIES—ALREADY. IF WE OBEY THOSE KILLERS AND DO NOTHING, THEN WE'RE DEAD ANYWAY.
REMEMBER WHEN HIV BROKE BIG? IT WAS THE "GAY" DISEASE.
THE GOVERNMENT DRAGGED ITS FEET UNTIL PEOPLE LIKE ME WERE DYING BY THE THOUSANDS HERE, AND THEN BY THE MILLIONS IN AFRICA.
A LOT OF GOOD PEOPLE SAID NOTHING. DID NOTHING. THAT MADE THEM COMPLICIT.
PERSONALLY, I'D RATHER GO DOWN FIGHTING THAN BY INACTION ALLOWING THEM TO WIN.
YOU'RE A JEW, MOSES. THIS IS A NEW HOLOCAUST. DON'T BE SO AFRAID FOR US THAT YOU LOSE YOUR HOPE THAT WE CAN WIN.
FUCK ME...

CHRIST ON A STICK, DE, HOW ARE YOU NOT GETTING THIS?
THAT KID IS COLLATERAL DAMAGE. SAD, YEAH. FUCKING TRAGIC. BUT THIS ISN'T A DEBATE.
WE.
CAN'T.
SAVE HER.
HE'S RIGHT, WE—
SHUT THE FUCK UP!
I'VE DEALT WITH INFECTED CHILDREN A LOT MORE THAN YOU HAVE, CHICK.
YEAH, AND REMEMBER WHAT HAPPENED LAST TIME? CONGO RING A BELL?
FUCK YOU FOR THROWING THAT IN MY FACE.
S.W.A.T
S.W.A.T
"I'M TAKING HER OUT OF HERE, CHICK, AND NEITHER YOU NOR ANYONE IS GOING TO STOP ME."

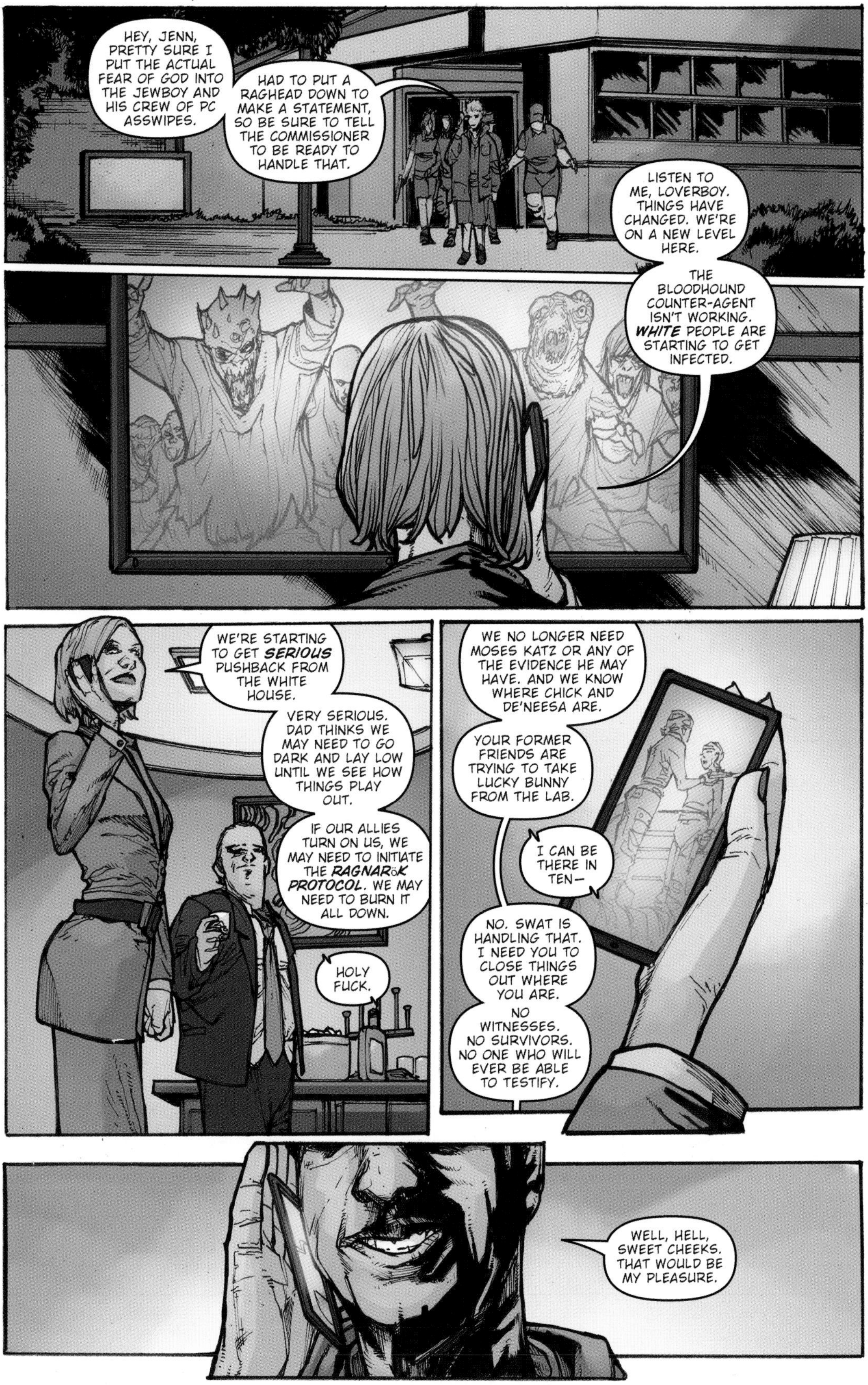
HEY, JENN, PRETTY SURE I PUT THE ACTUAL FEAR OF GOD INTO THE JEWBOY AND HIS CREW OF PC ASSWIPES.
HAD TO PUT A RAGHEAD DOWN TO MAKE A STATEMENT, SO BE SURE TO TELL THE COMMISSIONER TO BE READY TO HANDLE THAT.
LISTEN TO ME, LOVERBOY. THINGS HAVE CHANGED. WE'RE ON A NEW LEVEL HERE.
THE BLOODHOUND COUNTER-AGENT ISN'T WORKING. WHITE PEOPLE ARE STARTING TO GET INFECTED.
WE'RE STARTING TO GET SERIOUS PUSHBACK FROM THE WHITE HOUSE.
VERY SERIOUS. DAD THINKS WE MAY NEED TO GO DARK AND LAY LOW UNTIL WE SEE HOW THINGS PLAY OUT.
IF OUR ALLIES TURN ON US, WE MAY NEED TO INITIATE THE RAGNARöK PROTOCOL. WE MAY NEED TO BURN IT ALL DOWN.
HOLY FUCK.
WE NO LONGER NEED MOSES KATZ OR ANY OF THE EVIDENCE HE MAY HAVE. AND WE KNOW WHERE CHICK AND DE'NEESA ARE.
YOUR FORMER FRIENDS ARE TRYING TO TAKE LUCKY BUNNY FROM THE LAB.
I CAN BE THERE IN TEN—
NO. SWAT IS HANDLING THAT. I NEED YOU TO CLOSE THINGS OUT WHERE YOU ARE.
NO WITNESSES. NO SURVIVORS. NO ONE WHO WILL EVER BE ABLE TO TESTIFY.
WELL, HELL, SWEET CHEEKS. THAT WOULD BE MY PLEASURE.

YOUR OBJECTIONS ARE NOTED, CHICK. NOW SUIT UP, BECAUSE IN ONE MINUTE I'M OPENING THAT BASINET TO PUT BUNNY IN A SUIT.
DE'NEESA, I'M BEGGING YOU.
BEG WHILE SUITING UP. THIS IS HAPPENING.
"WE'VE BEEN HERE TOO LONG AS IT IS. WE MAY BE RUNNING OUT OF TIME."
WAIT, WAIT... WHAT ABOUT ME? IF YOU OPEN THAT BASINET—YOU'LL KILL ME.
DE... HAVE YOU LOST YOUR MIND? WE NEEDED HIM.
NOT ANYMORE. THE LITTLE GIRL IS WHAT WE NEED. LITTLE LUCKY BUNNY. THE PERFECT GIRL. THE CURE TO EVERYTHING.
NOW... ARE YOU GOING TO HELP ME OR NOT?

I CAN'T LET YOU DO THIS.
YOU LOSE YOUR BALLS? YOU WANT TO SHOOT ME TO PREVENT ME SAVING A KID?
MAYBE IT'S NOT JUST YOUR BALLS. MAYBE YOU'VE LOST YOUR SOUL.
SOMETHING'S WRONG WITH YOU, DE. YOU'RE NOT THINKING STRAIGHT.
MAYBE IT'S WHAT HAPPENED IN THE CONGO. MAYBE IT'S PTSD. EITHER WAY, I CAN'T LET YOU DO THIS.
I CAN'T.
THEN LET ME MAKE IT EASY FOR YOU. FIVE POUNDS OF PRESSURE ON THAT TRIGGER AND YOU'RE THE HERO. THAT'S WHAT YOU WANT TO BE, RIGHT?
WE BOTH HAVE GHOSTS HAUNTING US, CHICK. MINE HAUNT ME FOR MISTAKES I MADE TRYING TO SAVE PEOPLE. YOURS ARE FOR PEOPLE YOU DIDN'T NEED TO KILL, BUT DID BECAUSE IT MADE THE JOB EASIER. SIMPLER.
THIS IS PRETTY SIMPLE NOW. SHOOT ME OR HELP ME.
WE CAN LOAD THE BASINETS ON THIS. TAKE THEM OUT THE BACK AND HOTWIRE SOMETHING IN THE GARAGE.
FINE.
I'LL WAIT UNTIL YOU HAVE THE OTHER KIDS LOADED IN ONE VEHICLE. THEN I'LL GET BUNNY OUT IN ANOTHER.
FINE.
YOU'RE MAKING THE RIGHT CHOICE HERE.
FINE.

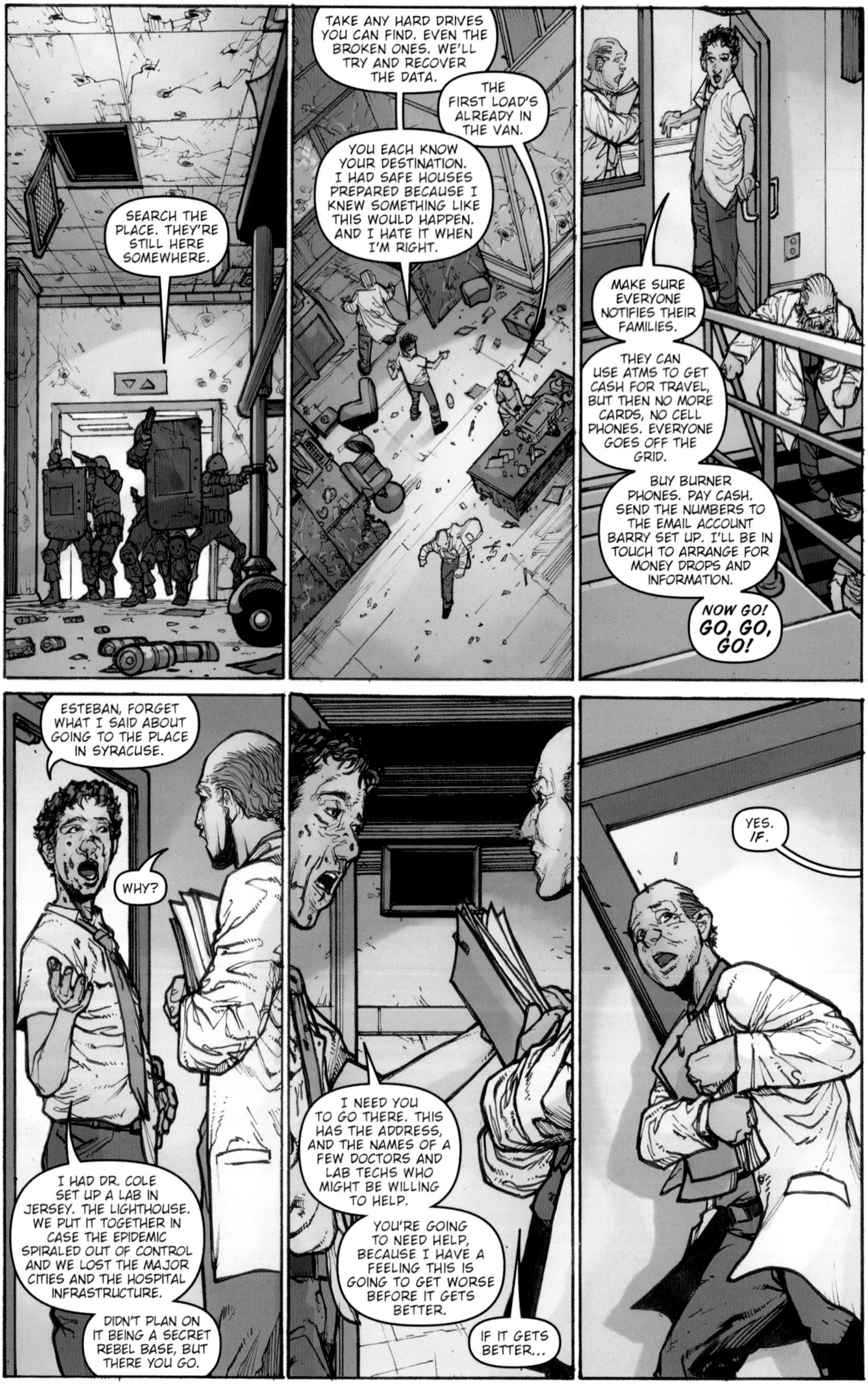
SEARCH THE PLACE. THEY'RE STILL HERE SOMEWHERE.
TAKE ANY HARD DRIVES YOU CAN FIND. EVEN THE BROKEN ONES. WE'LL TRY AND RECOVER THE DATA.
THE FIRST LOAD'S ALREADY IN THE VAN.
YOU EACH KNOW YOUR DESTINATION. I HAD SAFE HOUSES PREPARED BECAUSE I KNEW SOMETHING LIKE THIS WOULD HAPPEN. AND I HATE IT WHEN I'M RIGHT.
MAKE SURE EVERYONE NOTIFIES THEIR FAMILIES.
THEY CAN USE ATMS TO GET CASH FOR TRAVEL, BUT THEN NO MORE CARDS, NO CELL PHONES. EVERYONE GOES OFF THE GRID.
BUY BURNER PHONES. PAY CASH. SEND THE NUMBERS TO THE EMAIL ACCOUNT BARRY SET UP. I'LL BE IN TOUCH TO ARRANGE FOR MONEY DROPS AND INFORMATION.
NOW GO! GO, GO, GO!
ESTEBAN, FORGET WHAT I SAID ABOUT GOING TO THE PLACE IN SYRACUSE.
WHY?
I HAD DR. COLE SET UP A LAB IN JERSEY. THE LIGHTHOUSE. WE PUT IT TOGETHER IN CASE THE EPIDEMIC SPIRALED OUT OF CONTROL AND WE LOST THE MAJOR CITIES AND THE HOSPITAL INFRASTRUCTURE.
DIDN'T PLAN ON IT BEING A SECRET REBEL BASE, BUT THERE YOU GO.
I NEED YOU TO GO THERE. THIS HAS THE ADDRESS, AND THE NAMES OF A FEW DOCTORS AND LAB TECHS WHO MIGHT BE WILLING TO HELP.
YOU'RE GOING TO NEED HELP, BECAUSE I HAVE A FEELING THIS IS GOING TO GET WORSE BEFORE IT GETS BETTER.
IF IT GETS BETTER...
YES. *IF.*

PING
POKA-POKA-POKA
I'LL TRY AND HOLD THEM. GOD--
RUN!
KRAK
KRAK

PERFECT. HOTWIRE THIS MOTHERFUCKER LIKE I USED TO IN HIGH SCHOOL. GET THESE FREAKING KIDS BACK TO PANDEMICA.
MOSES IS GOING TO SHIT A FULL-GROWN ALLIGATOR WHEN I TELL HIM ABOUT THIS. AND COLE? CHRIST, THAT OL' BOY'S JUST GOING TO PLAIN STROKE OUT AND DIE.
YOU HAVE STEPPED IN THE SHIT, OLD SON. YOU SURELY HAVE.
LISTEN, MOSES, CALL ME AS SOON AS YOU GET THIS. AND I MEAN RIGHT AWAY.
DE'S GOING TOTALLY OFF THE RESERVATION HERE.
THERE'S THIS KID. SUPER INFECTED. SOME KIND OF FREAK. DE THINKS THE KID'S OUR ONLY SHOT AT A CURE.
MAYBE SHE IS, BUT THE ARK DOCTOR SOLD HER AS A THREAT ON THE LEVEL OF AN ASTEROID MADE OF EBOLA.
HATE TO SAY THIS, MAN, BUT I THINK WE MAY NEED TO—
NEED TO ***WHAT***, CHICK?
I LOVE YOU... BUT I ***KNEW*** I COULDN'T TRUST YOU.
I'M TRYING TO KEEP YOU FROM MAKING THE WORLD'S WORST MISTAKE.
YOU DON'T GET TO PLAY JUDGE, JURY, AND EXECUTIONER.
YEAH, WELL, YOU DON'T GET TO PLAY ***GOD***.
I'M NOT PLAYING GOD.
I'M BEING A HUMAN BEING.
WE'RE THE GOOD GUYS, CHICK. WE'RE SUPPOSED TO STOP PEOPLE FROM HURTING THE INNOCENT.
BULLSHIT. IT'S NOT THAT BLACK AND WHITE. AND YOU DAMN WELL KNOW IT.

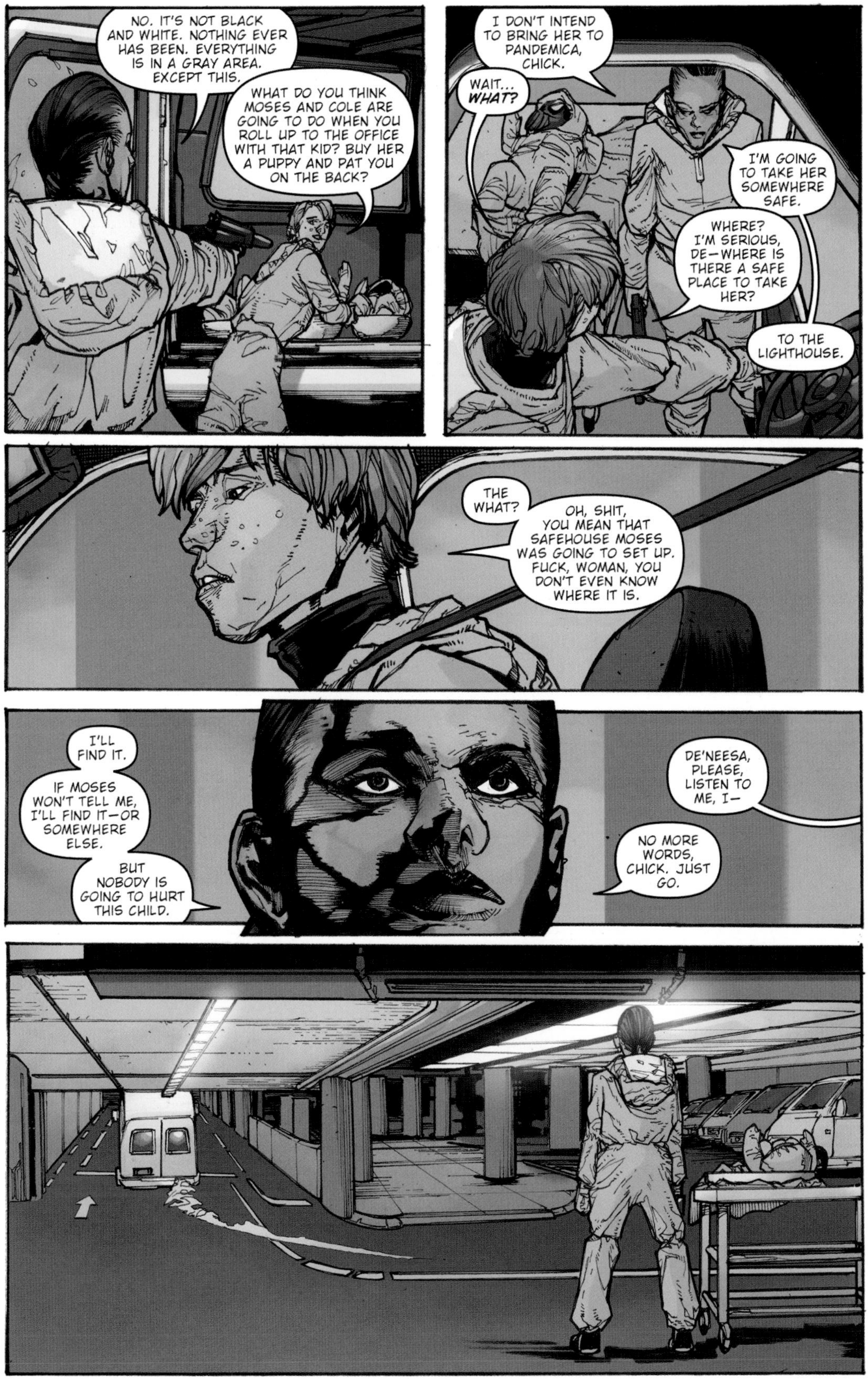
NO. IT'S NOT BLACK AND WHITE. NOTHING EVER HAS BEEN. EVERYTHING IS IN A GRAY AREA. EXCEPT THIS.
WHAT DO YOU THINK MOSES AND COLE ARE GOING TO DO WHEN YOU ROLL UP TO THE OFFICE WITH THAT KID? BUY HER A PUPPY AND PAT YOU ON THE BACK?
I DON'T INTEND TO BRING HER TO PANDEMICA, CHICK.
WAIT... *WHAT?*
I'M GOING TO TAKE HER SOMEWHERE SAFE.
WHERE? I'M SERIOUS, DE—WHERE IS THERE A SAFE PLACE TO TAKE HER?
TO THE LIGHTHOUSE.
THE WHAT?
OH, SHIT, YOU MEAN THAT SAFEHOUSE MOSES WAS GOING TO SET UP. FUCK, WOMAN, YOU DON'T EVEN KNOW WHERE IT IS.
I'LL FIND IT.
IF MOSES WON'T TELL ME, I'LL FIND IT—OR SOMEWHERE ELSE.
BUT NOBODY IS GOING TO HURT THIS CHILD.
DE'NEESA, PLEASE, LISTEN TO ME, I—
NO MORE WORDS, CHICK. JUST GO.

IT'S OKAY, LITTLE BUNNY.
I'LL TAKE CARE OF YOU.
AND I WON'T LET ANYONE HURT YOU.
I PROMISE.
POKA-POKA-POKA
KRAK
KRAK

SOON.
I dont have much time. They're close. Get to the Lighthouse. Hurry.
38.9330°N, 74.9606°W
We're running out of time.
M.K.

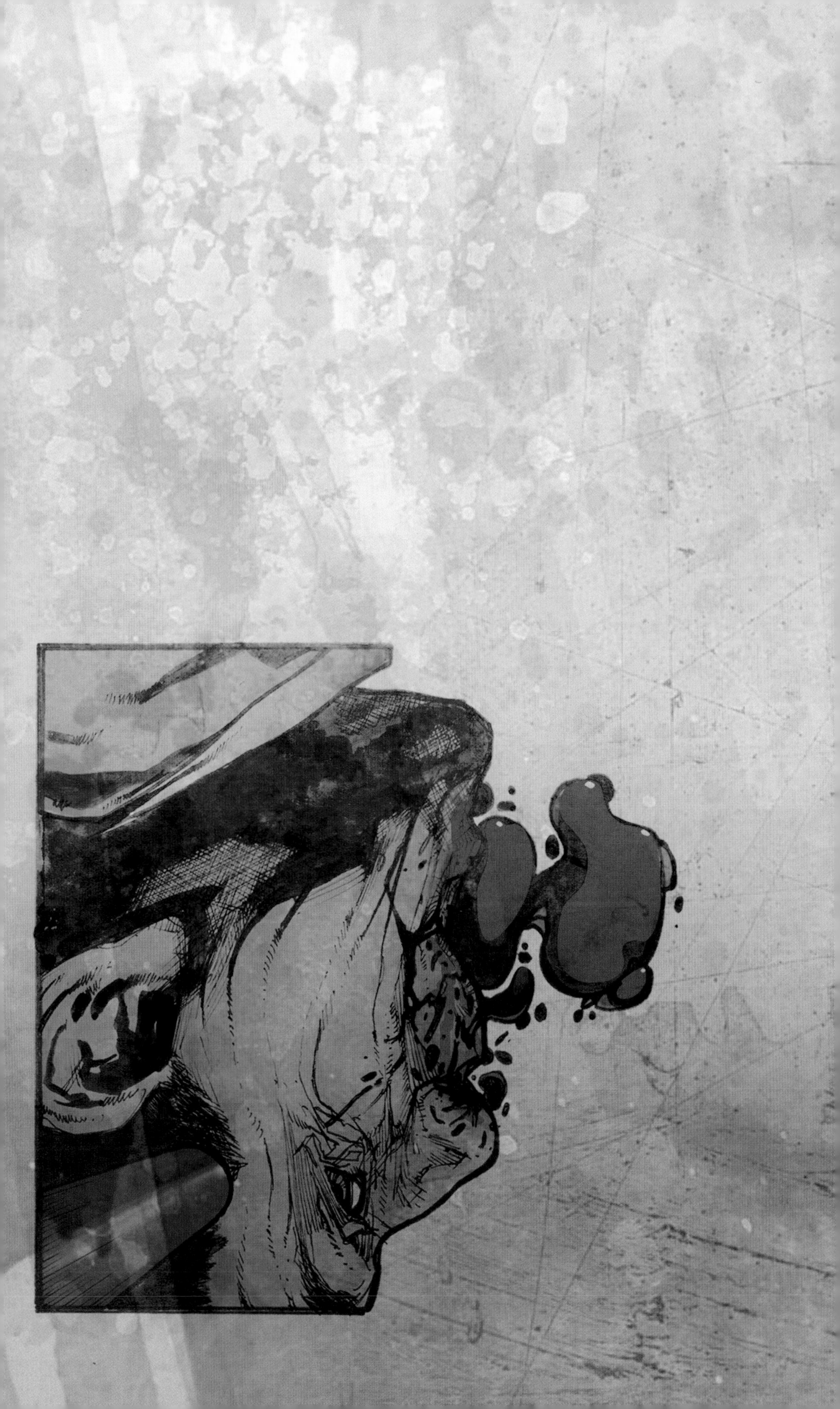

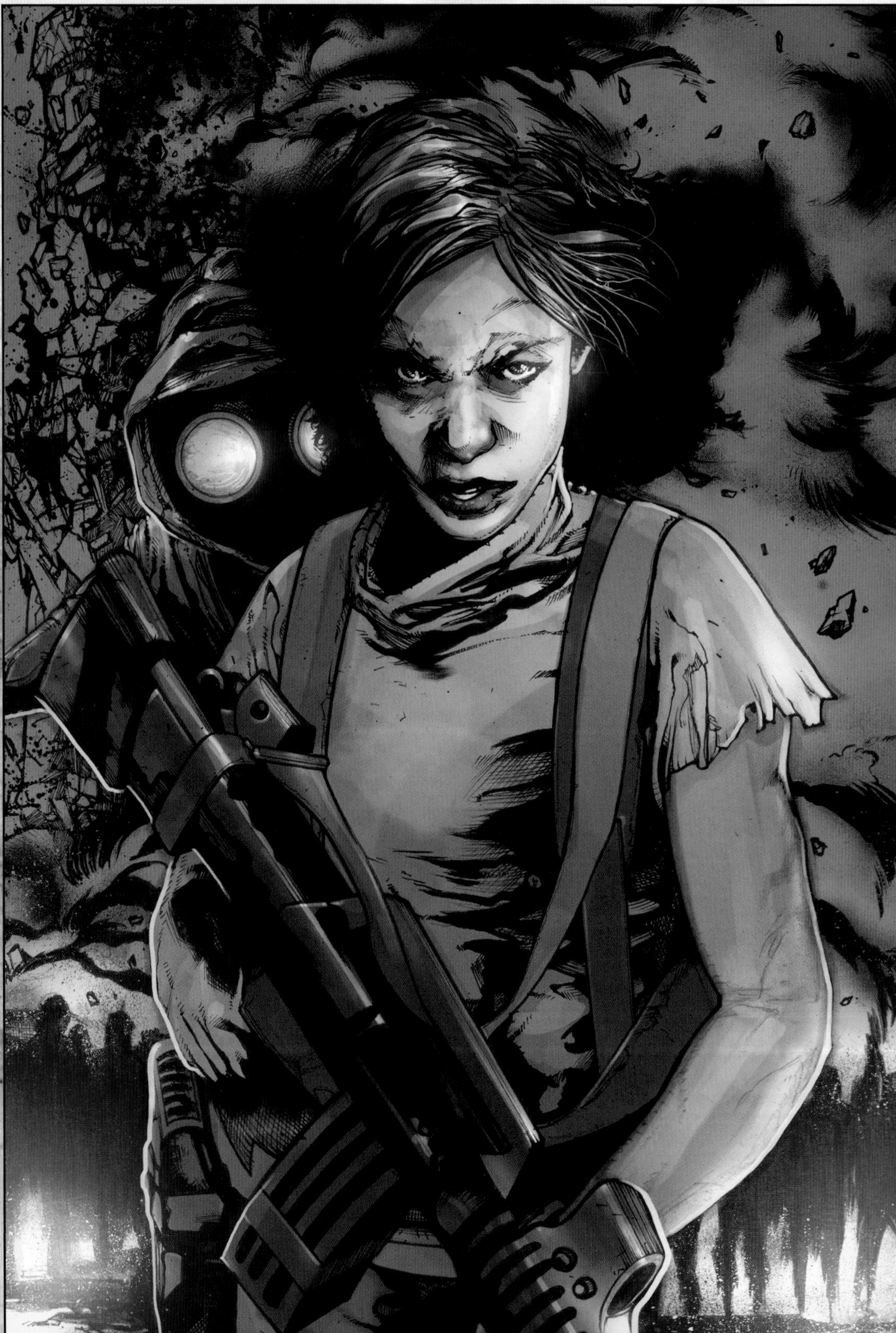
IRONHED
2019

ART BY **ALEX SANCHEZ** COLORS BY **JAY FOTOS**

NOT SURE WHAT'S WORSE.
THE ARK MANIACS RELEASING ETHNIC-SPECIFIC BIOWEAPONS...
...OR TESTING THEM OUT FIRST ON BABIES.
THE WORLD IS BROKEN.
NONE OF THE PIECES FIT ANYMORE.
MAYBE THEY NEVER HAVE, AND I DIDN'T NOTICE.
BUT I'M GOING TO CHANGE THAT.
AUNTIE DE WILL BE RIGHT BACK.

IF YOU'RE REALLY UPS, THEN I'M BEYONCÉ.
IF YOU'RE HERE, THEN SOMEONE'S UPSTAIRS CAUSING TROUBLE WITH PANDEMICA. WITH MY *FRIENDS*.
TELL ME OR DIE.
OR BOTH.
SPECIAL DELIVERY, MOTHER-FUCKERS!

KILLING HAS GOTTEN EASY.
I PROBABLY SHOULD BE WORRIED ABOUT THAT.
JESUS FUCKING CHRIST!
POKA-POKA-POKA-POKA
I'M NOT.
THE FUCK GOT INTO HER? THAT BITCH HAS LOST HER SHIT.
KA-BOOM
OWW. FUCK.

DAMN, MOSES... YOU'RE A MESS.
UHHH...
DON'T DIE ON ME YET. DON'T YOU DARE. WE HAVE WORK TO DO.
OOOF!
—LUCKY BUNNY. THAT'S HER IN THE BACK.
AND YEAH, SHE HAS EVERY SINGLE DISEASE KNOWN TO MAN.
AT LEAST, ALL THE REALLY BAD ONES.
BUT SHE'S ALIVE, AND I NEED TO GET HER TO OUR LAB TO FIGURE OUT WHY. HOW. BECAUSE I THINK SHE'S NOT ONLY THE ANSWER TO ARKS' EUGENICS BULLSHIT...
...I THINK SHE'S GOING TO SAVE THE WHOLE WORLD FROM ITSELF.
YOU'RE CIRCLING THE DRAIN, MOSES. CAN'T TAKE ANY RISKS STAYING WITH YOU. I HAVE TO DROP YOU AT THE HOSPITAL.
...IT'S... OKAY...
...CHICK'S WRONG... KEEP THE... BUNNY... SAFE...

I WILL. I SWEAR IT. BUT WHAT DO I DO?
EVERYONE WILL... WANT TO FIND HER.
THE GALTONS. THE GOVERNMENT.
CHICK...
...GOD... I'M FADING OUT...
...SAFE... PROMISE...
MOSES... I WILL. I PROMISE.
BUT WHERE? I'VE ALREADY TRIED THREE SAFE HOUSES. THEY'VE BEEN COMPROMISED.
TWO OTHERS ARE UNDER SURVEILLANCE. I WAS GOING TO TRY THE ONE DOWN IN PHILLY NEXT.
YOU MUST... GET HER TO...
...LIGHTHOUSE...
I KNOW, BUT WHERE IS IT? IS THAT THE ONE IN PHILLY?
...LIGHTHOUSE... PHILADELPHIA... SAFE...
GOT IT! THANKS. GOD BE WITH YOU.
NO, DE... LISTEN...
...LIGHTHOUSE IS IN CAPE MAY.
DON'T GO TO PHILLY. LOVERBOY KNOWS ABOUT IT.
HOSPITAL
EMERGENCY
NOT SAFE... GOD... PLEASE...

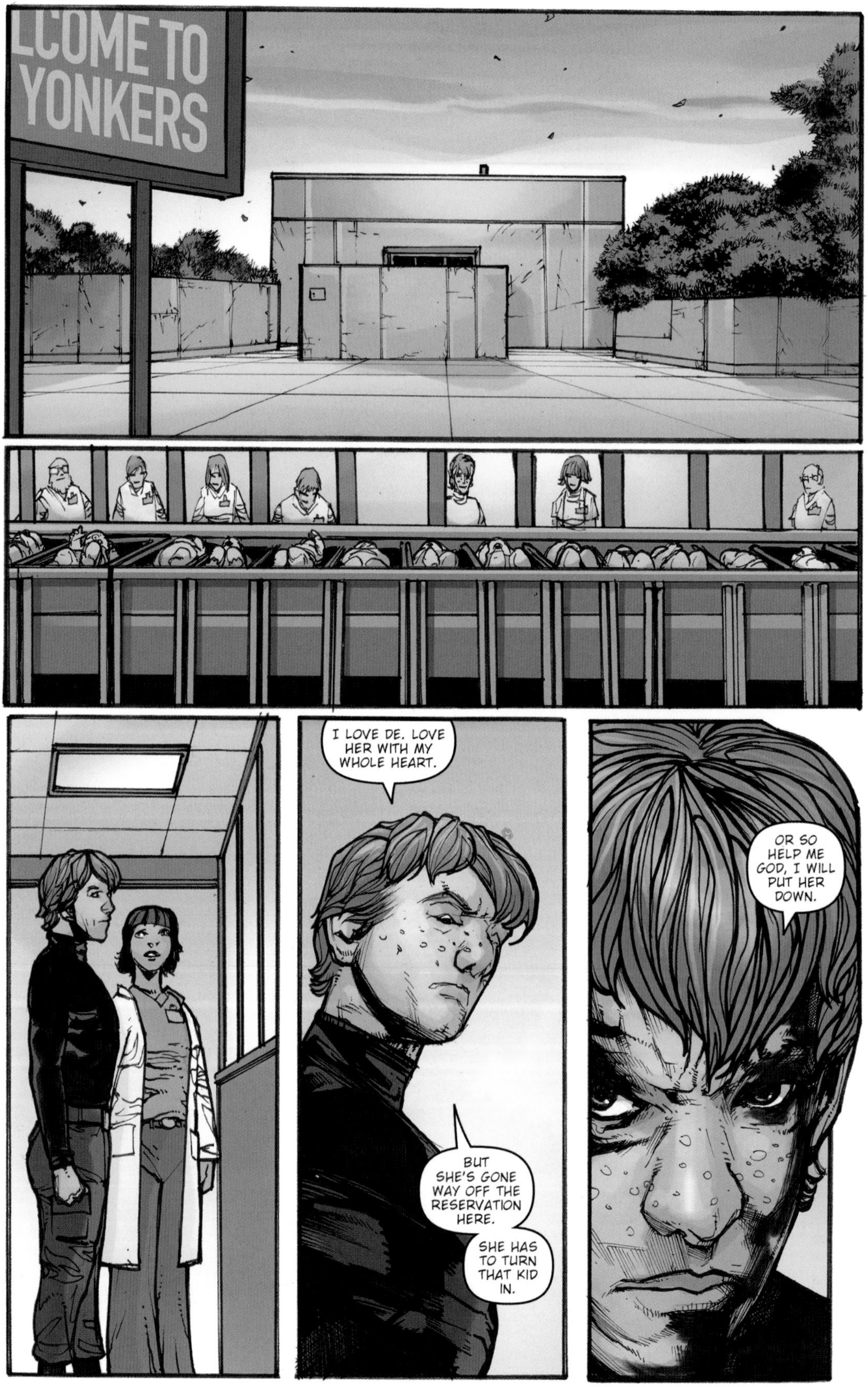
LCOME TO
YONKERS
I LOVE DE. LOVE HER WITH MY WHOLE HEART.
BUT SHE'S GONE WAY OFF THE RESERVATION HERE.
SHE HAS TO TURN THAT KID IN.
OR SO HELP ME GOD, I WILL PUT HER DOWN.

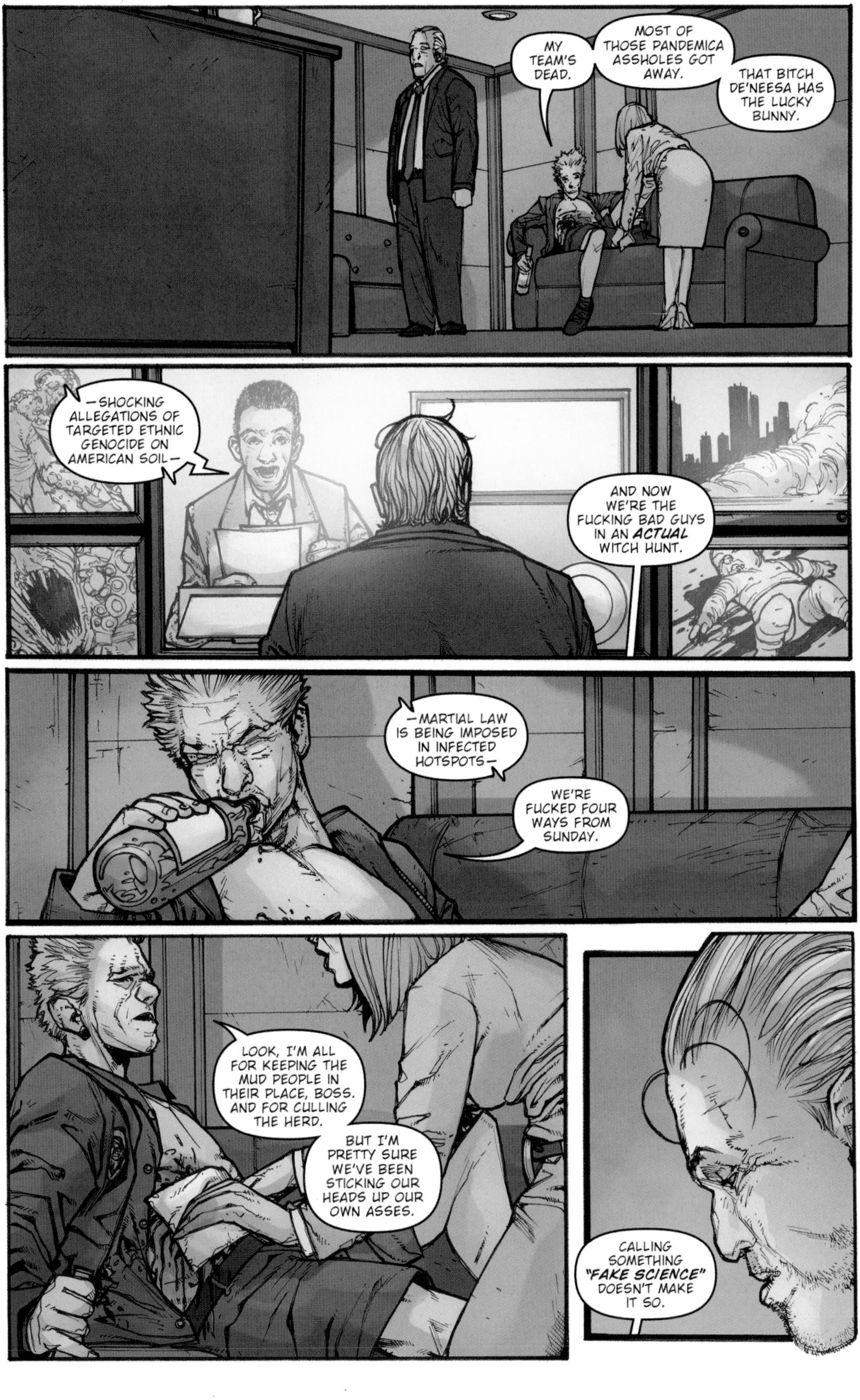
MY TEAM'S DEAD.
MOST OF THOSE PANDEMICA ASSHOLES GOT AWAY.
THAT BITCH DE'NEESA HAS THE LUCKY BUNNY.
—SHOCKING ALLEGATIONS OF TARGETED ETHNIC GENOCIDE ON AMERICAN SOIL—
AND NOW WE'RE THE FUCKING BAD GUYS IN AN ACTUAL WITCH HUNT.
—MARTIAL LAW IS BEING IMPOSED IN INFECTED HOTSPOTS—
WE'RE FUCKED FOUR WAYS FROM SUNDAY.
LOOK, I'M ALL FOR KEEPING THE MUD PEOPLE IN THEIR PLACE, BOSS. AND FOR CULLING THE HERD.
BUT I'M PRETTY SURE WE'VE BEEN STICKING OUR HEADS UP OUR OWN ASSES.
CALLING SOMETHING "FAKE SCIENCE" DOESN'T MAKE IT SO.

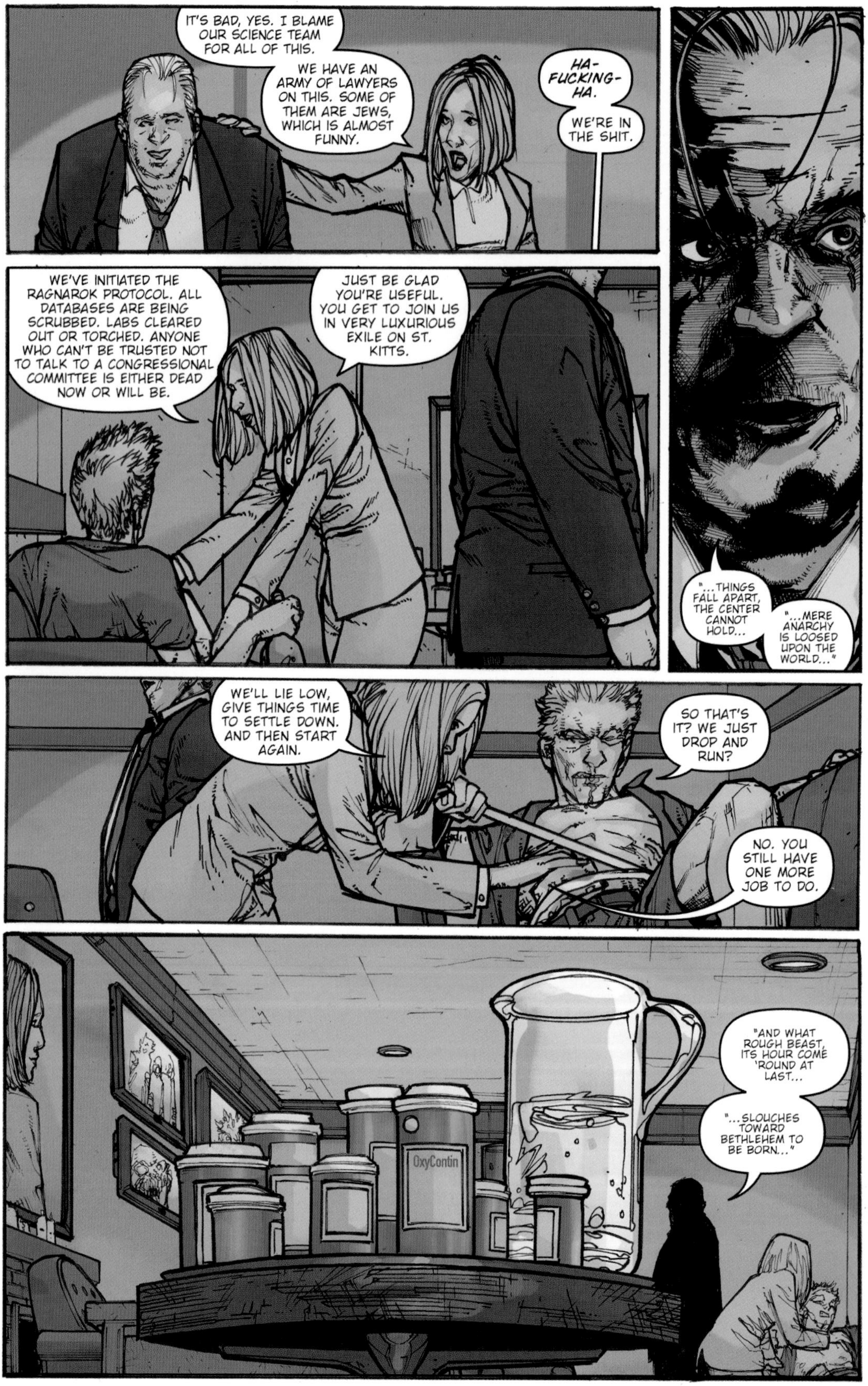
IT'S BAD, YES. I BLAME OUR SCIENCE TEAM FOR ALL OF THIS.
WE HAVE AN ARMY OF LAWYERS ON THIS. SOME OF THEM ARE JEWS, WHICH IS ALMOST FUNNY.
HA-FUCKING-HA.
WE'RE IN THE SHIT.
WE'VE INITIATED THE RAGNAROK PROTOCOL. ALL DATABASES ARE BEING SCRUBBED. LABS CLEARED OUT OR TORCHED. ANYONE WHO CAN'T BE TRUSTED NOT TO TALK TO A CONGRESSIONAL COMMITTEE IS EITHER DEAD NOW OR WILL BE.
JUST BE GLAD YOU'RE USEFUL. YOU GET TO JOIN US IN VERY LUXURIOUS EXILE ON ST. KITTS.
"...THINGS FALL APART, THE CENTER CANNOT HOLD...
"...MERE ANARCHY IS LOOSED UPON THE WORLD..."
WE'LL LIE LOW, GIVE THINGS TIME TO SETTLE DOWN. AND THEN START AGAIN.
SO THAT'S IT? WE JUST DROP AND RUN?
NO. YOU STILL HAVE ONE MORE JOB TO DO.
OxyContin
"AND WHAT ROUGH BEAST, ITS HOUR COME 'ROUND AT LAST...
"...SLOUCHES TOWARD BETHLEHEM TO BE BORN..."

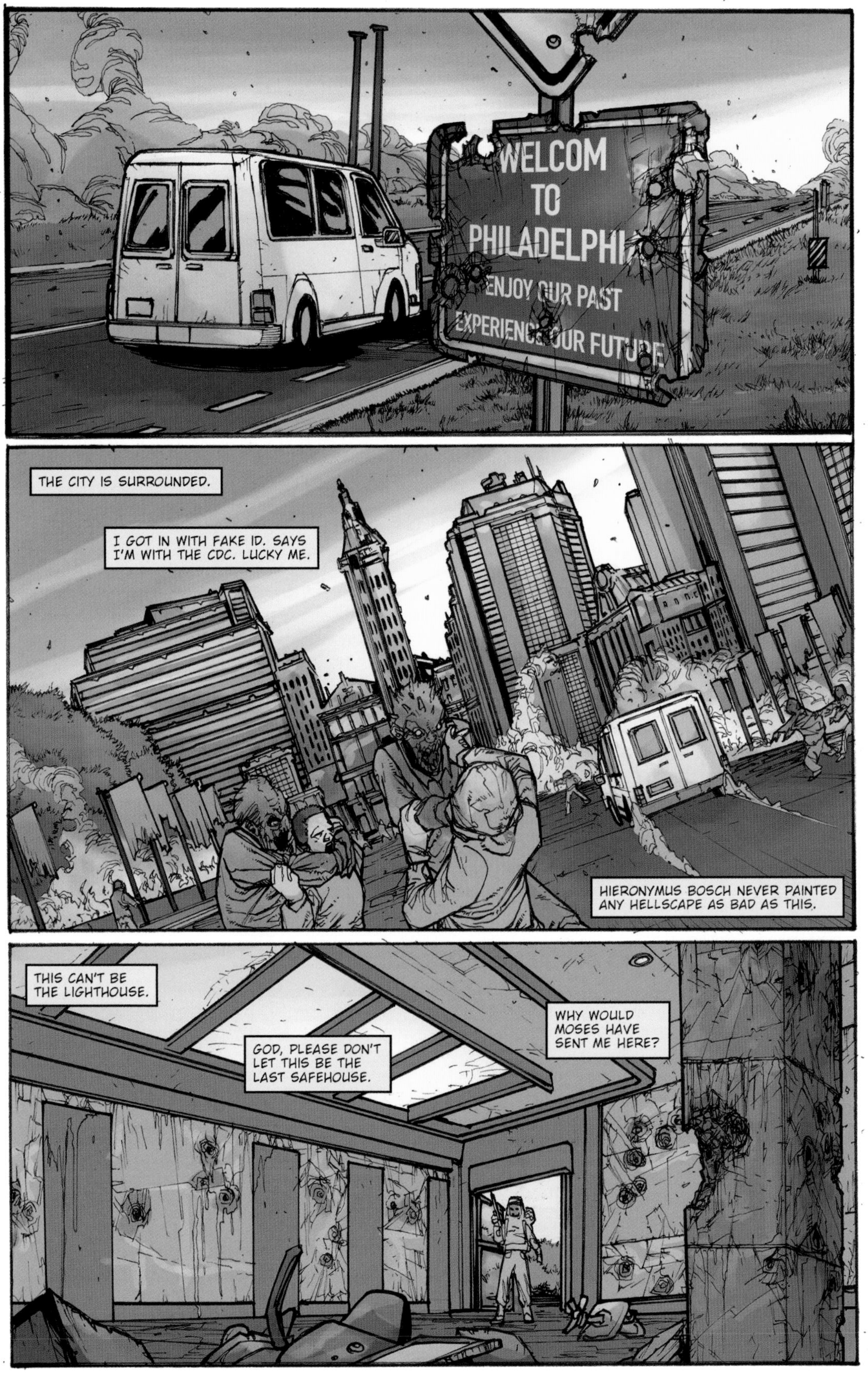
WELCOM
TO
PHILADELPHI
ENJOY OUR PAST
EXPERIENCE OUR FUTURE
THE CITY IS SURROUNDED.
I GOT IN WITH FAKE ID. SAYS I'M WITH THE CDC. LUCKY ME.
HIERONYMUS BOSCH NEVER PAINTED ANY HELLSCAPE AS BAD AS THIS.
THIS CAN'T BE THE LIGHTHOUSE.
GOD, PLEASE DON'T LET THIS BE THE LAST SAFEHOUSE.
WHY WOULD MOSES HAVE SENT ME HERE?

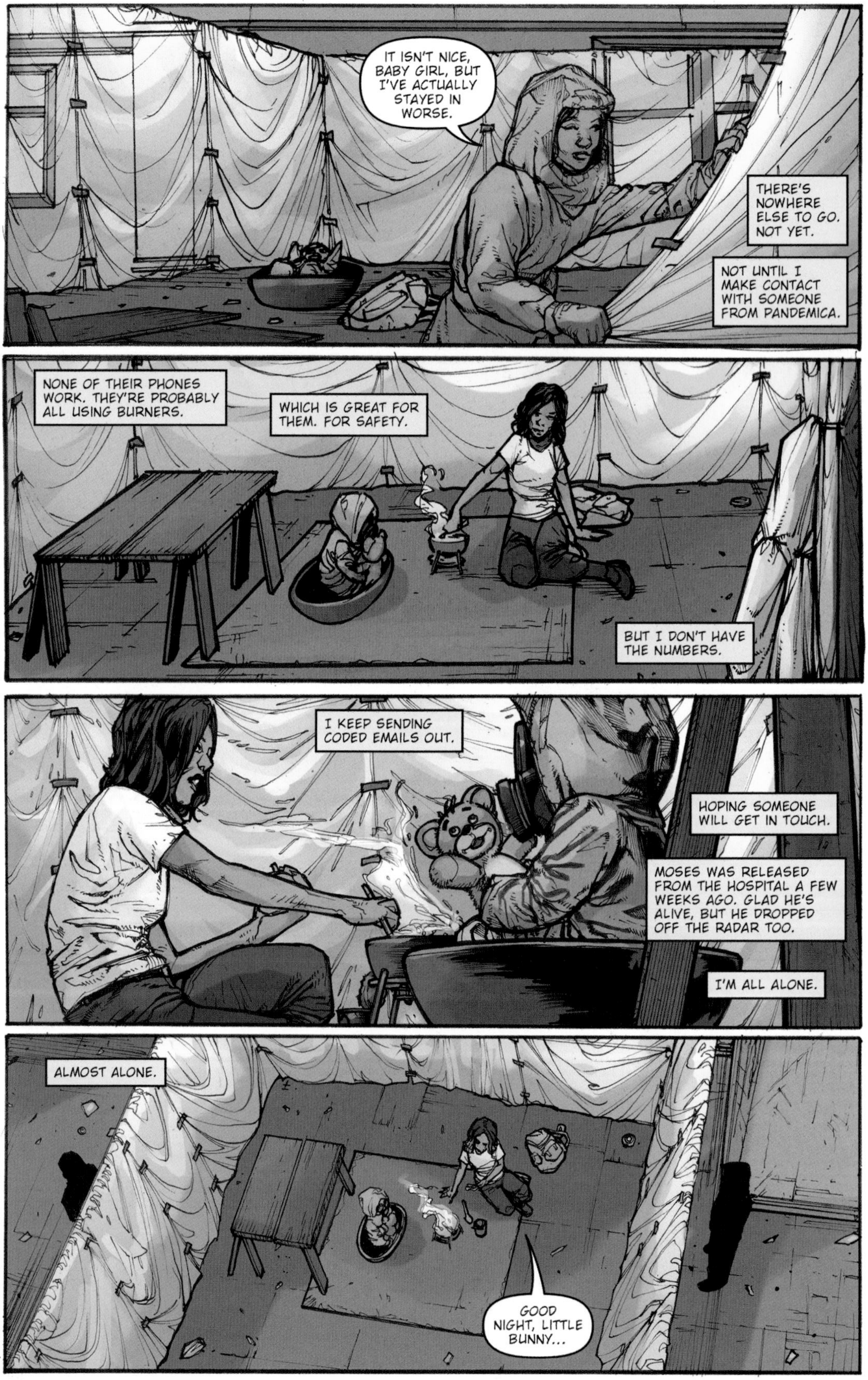
IT ISN'T NICE, BABY GIRL, BUT I'VE ACTUALLY STAYED IN WORSE.
THERE'S NOWHERE ELSE TO GO. NOT YET.
NOT UNTIL I MAKE CONTACT WITH SOMEONE FROM PANDEMICA.
NONE OF THEIR PHONES WORK. THEY'RE PROBABLY ALL USING BURNERS.
WHICH IS GREAT FOR THEM. FOR SAFETY.
BUT I DON'T HAVE THE NUMBERS.
I KEEP SENDING CODED EMAILS OUT.
HOPING SOMEONE WILL GET IN TOUCH.
MOSES WAS RELEASED FROM THE HOSPITAL A FEW WEEKS AGO. GLAD HE'S ALIVE, BUT HE DROPPED OFF THE RADAR TOO.
I'M ALL ALONE.
ALMOST ALONE.
GOOD NIGHT, LITTLE BUNNY...

...WITH THE SUICIDE OF KARL GALTON, THE FOCUS OF THE INVESTIGATION HAS STALLED.
PHILADELPHIA REMAINS UNDER INDEFINITE MARTIAL LAW WITH THE MUTATIONS CONTAINED BUT NOT CONTROLLED.
REPORTS OF MARAUDING GANGS AND LOOTING ARE COMMON, BUT THE AREA IS STILL DEEMED A HOT ZONE.
THE ACLU HAS ACCUSED THE WHITE HOUSE OF USING THE QUARANTINE TO SIMPLY LET THE INFECTED DIE OFF RATHER THAN TRY AND TREAT THE TENS OF THOUSANDS OF THOSE WHO ARE SICK.
HELLO?
GOD, IT'S REALLY YOU! DE, IT'S—
HUSH! NO NAMES. I KNOW WHO YOU ARE. ARE YOU SAFE?
YES. AND I'VE BEEN IN TOUCH WITH... THE BOSS. HE'S SAFE, TOO.
MESSED UP, BUT OKAY. HE SAID HE TRIED TO WARN YOU ABOUT PHILLY.
YEAH. THAT WAS FOR SHIT, AND NOW I'M STUCK HERE.
I HAVE NO IDEA WHERE THE LIGHTHOUSE IS. MAYBE THE BOSS WAS JUST DELIRIOUS.
DO YOU STILL HAVE THE, UM, KID?
YES.
AND SHE'S STILL HEALTHY? EVEN WITH EVERYTHING?
YES.

LOOK... THE BOSS HAS A WAY IN AND OUT OF PHILLY.
WON'T TELL ANY OF US HOW HE MANAGES IT.
HE'S BEEN LOOKING FOR YOU.
I CAN'T **BE** FOUND.
NO JOKE. POINT IS, HE HAS THE INFO ABOUT THE LIGHTHOUSE AND WANTS TO GET IT TO YOU.
HE DOESN'T TRUST PHONES. NOT EVEN BURNERS. HE'S TOTALLY PARANOID.
HE SHOULD BE.
I USED TO TRUST PEOPLE. I DON'T ANYMORE.
LOOK, I KNOW YOU'RE PARANOID ABOUT SHARING INFO ON THE PHONE, BUT THESE ARE BURNERS. THEY'RE ***UNTRACEABLE.***
NOTHING IS UNTRACEABLE. NO MATTER HOW CAREFUL YOU'RE BEING, BE ***MORE*** CAREFUL.
OKAY... BUT IF I CAN GET INFORMATION O THE LIGHTHOUS HOW DO I GET IT TO YOU?
I DON'T SUPPOSE... YOUR, ***UM, EX*** IS AN OPTION?
NO.
FUCK.
LOOK, I'LL TEXT YOU WITH A DROP SITE. ONCE YOU GET IT, IMMEDIATELY DESTROY THE SIM CARD AND THROW THE PHONE AWAY.
OKAY, BUT—
CLICK

IN THE MILITARY, ONE OF THE MOST VALUABLE SKILLS IS PATIENCE.
YOU NEVER WANT TO MAKE A MOVE WITHOUT INTEL OR OPTIONS.
DOUBLY SO IN THE KIND OF SPECOPS CREWS I RAN WITH.
BUT WAITING IS A BITCH. IT'S A MONSTER.
OUTSIDE OF THIS PLACE THERE ARE MONSTERS IN THE STREETS.
ACTUAL MONSTERS.
AND KILLERS IN UNIFORMS. WEARING BADGES.
WE'RE STANDING ON THE EDGE, AND THE ABYSS IS CALLING.
I ALMOST WANT TO LET IT TAKE ME.
ALMOST.
RRYNNG
I HAVE IT.
THE LIGHTHOUSE LOCATION. THE BOSS LEFT INFORMATION FOR YOU.
BUT IT'S ALL THE WAY ON THE OTHER SIDE OF THE CITY.
BEST HE COULD DO BEFORE HE... WELL... HE WENT DARK AFTER THAT.
I'LL TEXT YOU THE ADDRESS.

COME ON, BABY GIRL. LET'S GO GET YOU FIXED.
LET'S GO SAVE THE WORLD.

I dont have
much time.
They're close.
to the Lighthouse
Hurry.
38.9930°N
74.9600°W
We're running out
of time.
M.K.
COME ON, DE. MAKE THIS RIGHT.
OUFF!
I LOVE YOU, BABY.
I TRUST YOU.
MAKE THIS RIGHT.

POKA-
POKA-
POKA-
POKA
UGGGH!
POKA
KRA-KOW
KRACK
FUCKING DIE!
KAPOOM

YOU RUINED EVERYTHING, YOU HALF-BLACK BITCH.
FUCKING *EVERYTHING*.
NOW I'M GOING TO RUIN YOU.
I'M GOING TO MAKE YOU BEG FOR IT!
POK
COME... ON... BABY GIRL...
MOMMY'S GONNA... TAKE YOU... HOME...

38.9330° N, 74.9606° W
AN ACTUAL LIGHTHOUSE. FUCK ME.
CHRIST! DE!
SHE'S HURT.
THANK GOD... HER HAZMAT SUIT'S INTACT.
IT'S ALL TRUE. HER BODY HAS BALANCED EVERYTHING. SHE'S A MIRACLE.
HER BLOOD... GOD DAMN... SHE IS THE CURE...
SEE, BABY GIRL.
MOMMY SAID SHE'D... TAKE YOU...
...HOME.

ART BY **ALEX SANCHEZ**

ART BY **ALEX SANCHEZ**

ART BY **ALEX SANCHEZ**

ART BY **ALEX SANCHEZ**

IRONHED
2019

ART BY **ALEX SANCHEZ**

ART BY **ESTEBAN SALINAS**

JONATHAN MABERRY

JONATHAN MABERRY is a *New York Times* bestselling and multiple Bram Stoker Award-winning author, anthology editor, comic book writer, magazine feature writer, playwright, content creator and writing teacher/lecturer. He was named one of the Top Ten Horror Writers alive today. His books have been sold in more than thirty countries.

Jonathan's young adult fiction includes the ***Rot & Ruin*** series (winner of multiple Bram Stoker awards). His adult fiction includes the ***Joe Ledger*** thrillers from St. Martin's Griffin (***Patient Zero*** also was a Bram Stoker award winner). His zombie novels ***Dead of Night*** (2013) and ***Fall of Night*** (2014) are also in development for film. Jonathan is also the author of several award-winning nonfiction books on the folklore of vampires and the pop-culture phenomenon of zombies.

Jonathan is the editor and co-author of ***V-WARS***, a shared-world vampire anthology from IDW now adapted to TV and streaming on Netflix.

Jonathan, his wife, Sara Jo, to whom he dedicates all of his published works, and their dog, Rosie, live in Del Mar, California.

Visit his website/blog and sign up for his free newsletter at *www.jonathanmaberry.com*